"Even the bravest heart falters at the edge of the forest after nightfall, for something primal within remembers the ancient predator that lurks in the shadows."

~ Terry Goodkind, Sword of Truth

Jackolantern

Camp Fire Stories – Book Two

R E Barringham

ISBN: Paperback: 978-0-6457543-6-0
             eBook   978-0-6457543-7-7

Also by R E Barringham

Playing For Real
Two Weeks In Corfu
Stand By Me
What Goes Around Comes Around
Mackarb - Campfire Story Book 1
Magenta - Campfire Story Book 3

How to Quit Smoking
How to Write an Article in 15 Minutes
Goodbye Writers Block
7 Day eBook Writing and Publishing System
Living the Laptop Lifestyle
Mission Critical For Life
The Monthly Challenge Writing Series
12 Month Writing Challenge
How To Have More Money
Stop Procrastinating

Halloween

Gerald hated Halloween. Always had. Now he hated it even more, but for a whole new reason.

He'd just arrived home from work and was sitting in his car on the driveway, waiting for the electric garage door to finish opening so that he could drive in when he saw it. Someone had carved a face in a pumpkin and left it on his front porch.

It was probably one of his neighbours doing it as a joke. He'd told them multiple times over the years that he hated Halloween, so they all knew it. He always locked his front gate on Halloween night so that trick-or-treaters couldn't get in, and he had security cameras set up so if any of the little brats decided to leave a 'trick' because they didn't get a treat, he'd have all the evidence he needed to show the police.

Oh yes, he knew how to completely disengage from all the malarky that happened on Halloween night. It was just a shame that he couldn't disengage from it when he was a kid.

When he was younger, his parents forced Gerald and his two sisters to go out trick or treating. His two younger sisters were happy to do it, but Gerald hated it, but his protests always fell on deaf ears. His parents could never understand why he didn't want to do it, and not only ignored his pleas but also ignored his lack-lustre involvement and the look of disgust and anger on his face as he was forced to knock on door after door after door, dressed in a not-scary-at-all, ridiculous costume.

He didn't understand why he was coerced into participating year after year in something that wasn't even a big deal here in Australia.

Unfortunately, Gerald lived in Mount Eden, a small town in the Sunshine Coast Hinterland in Queensland. It was part of the Glass House Mountains area. Mount Eden (inaptly named because it was too small to be classed as a mountain) was one of the few places in the country where Halloween was a 'thing' and the so-called community-minded folks liked to get involved in any way that everyone could get together and have fun.

Ugh! None of the activities in Eden were fun, not to Gerald. He despised them all, especially on Halloween when he had to endure wearing a stupid costume and engaging with neighbours just to get a bag full of candy that he didn't even want. Treats like that were usually called lollies, but on Halloween, everyone used the American term candy. The day after Halloween, he would show his disdain for his 'candy' treats by depositing the whole bag of them in the wheelie bin outside.

When he turned 13, he said no to his parents about their Halloween nonsense and flatly refused to go.

Now as an adult, living in his own house he didn't have to put up with Halloween nonsense from anyone. Mostly, no one where he lived bothered with Halloween anyway, except a few hopeful teenagers who'd sometimes try their luck knocking on doors, and the odd, pushy parents who walked their kids around the neighbourhood, disturbing everyone.

That's why, as a precaution, Gerald kept his front gate locked on Halloween night, with a padlock and chain, not just to keep trick-or-treaters out, but also because he didn't like strangers on his property at any time. Halloween seemed to be a time when people seemed to deem it acceptable to walk up to his front door uninvited and expect to be rewarded for doing so.

Gerald valued his privacy. His security cameras were installed prominently to deter people from coming onto his property and to keep it secure while he was at work. He also had his yard fully fenced, with clear physical boundary lines.

His house was a neat wooden structure. Looking at it from the street, the driveway and garage were on the right, the front bedroom window was on the left, and the front porch was in the middle.

There was a metal chain-link fence spanning the front of the property, with a large, sliding electric gate in front of the driveway and a pedestrian gate in the middle opposite the porch. There was no path between the pedestrian gate and the porch because Gerald felt it would only encourage visitors. His whole yard, front to back was neat, with only a couple of trees and a tidy lawn that was mown regularly.

The fastidious and minimal neatness of the front façade of his property was now disrupted by the sudden appearance of the large, orange Jackolantern.

He was surprised that anyone would have put it there given that they could hardly miss seeing the obvious security cameras. Perhaps they thought they were dummy cameras. Either way, Gerald didn't want Halloween 'gifts' or any involvement in Halloween at all. It was just less than 2 weeks until the dreaded day and the pumpkin would probably be rotting by then anyway. So, what was the point? Unless they simply wanted to annoy him.

Seeing it there just reminded him of his Halloween-filled childhood, with a pumpkin on the porch, decorations in the garden, trick or treating, street parties afterwards, everybody into each other's business and people making snippy comments about each other behind their backs and being accused of being weird or rude if you didn't want to get involved in all these things.

Just thinking about it all made him physically shudder and glad he'd escaped it all. Gerald had moved away from Mount Eden 9 years ago. He got a job in the city of Brisbane and rented an apartment there until he'd saved enough money to buy a house of his own in one of the suburbs.

Gerald was a 35-year-old computer coder, and worked for a large company that wrote code for apps, games and software programs. He was one of their top coders, probably because he loved the work. He had his own office at the company while most of the other staff had a small cubicle in the bullpen. But he needed the office so that he didn't get disturbed when he was working. Most of the codes he worked on were extremely complicated, so he needed long stretches of uninterrupted time.

Today had been a tiring day because he'd spent most of it in meetings, which was the hardest, and most boring, work of all. He wanted to go home, hide away in his house, and do nothing.

But he'd come home to the Jackolantern, just one more thing he had to deal with before he could relax.

He parked the car in the garage and walked straight over to the pumpkin, picked it up, walked across the front of the house to the wheelie bins at the other side, lifted the lid of the general waste bin and dropped it in. It fell with a heavy thud.

The pumpkin was big. Gerald was surprised by how heavy it was but didn't want to show it as he carried it purposefully to the bin. As he dropped it in, he realised that had it been any bigger, it would have been too wide to fit in the bin. He was grateful for the large bag of rubbish that was already in the bin, which provided a softer landing for the pumpkin, otherwise the weight of it might have split the bottom.

Whoever had carved it hadn't done it very well, because as he was carrying it, he noticed that they'd slipped with the knife so one side of its upper lip was crooked where a jagged piece had been nicked out.

He bet that they were watching him. Quite a few of his neighbours, and their kids, were out as he drove up the street. October was one of the warmer months, the middle of spring, so there were often more people outside at this time of year.

To make himself look unconcerned about the uninvited pumpkin, Gerald didn't look around as he walked back towards the open garage, wiping his hands together exaggeratedly as he went.

There was a metal sink in the garage on the far wall next to the door leading into the house. He pressed the remote control on the side wall as he walked in, and the big metal door hummed and rattled down behind him as he walked across the concrete floor. By the time he reached the sink, the door was closed. Gerald washed his hands. The small electric timer light on the door controller on the ceiling provided just enough light for him to be able to see what he was doing. He dried his hands on the small towel hanging from a shelf above the sink, and then unlocked the connecting door and went into the house, locking the door behind him and giving the handle one quick rattle to doubly make sure it was locked.

He felt satisfied that he'd got one up on the pumpkin carver by getting rid of the pumpkin straight away and showing his contempt by throwing it in the garbage where it belonged.

He'd spent his whole life trying to stay away from all the Halloween malarky, which was why he couldn't understand why anyone would try to engage him in it. Their arrogance of thinking it was okay to come into his yard and leave a Jackolantern on his porch annoyed him.

It was a stark reminder that he was once again stuck in the middle of all the cult stupidity surrounding Halloween. Just like Christmas and Easter, it was an annual waste of time that was hard to avoid. Everyone wanted to throw themselves completely into these so-called 'special times,' yet if you were to ask them why, and Gerald often did, they didn't understand it themselves, but they're happy to blindly go along with it anyway.

And now here it was again. Nearly two weeks until the dreaded Halloween night and already the stupidity had started.

But no more. He'd gotten rid of the badly carved pumpkin, even going out later that evening and throwing a bag of kitchen rubbish into the bin on top of it, so that should be the end of the Halloween nonsense.

He hoped.

The Pumpkin

The following evening, Gerald drove onto the driveway, clicked the remote controls (one to open the garage door in front of him and one to close the gate behind) and waited.

Looking towards the front porch, his back stiffened, and he took a deep, inward breath when he saw another craved pumpkin sitting there.

Suddenly, it felt like the garage door couldn't open fast enough. He wanted to drive in quickly and then get rid of the pumpkin.

As soon as the door opened fully, he drove the car in faster than he ever had before and had to hit the brakes so quickly that his tyres made a small screech noise.

He got out of the car, slamming the door as hard as he could and stormed over to the front porch. He reached out to grab the pumpkin, intending to march it over to the bin and throw it in. But he stopped.

When he looked at the pumpkin's face, he realised it was the same one that he'd thrown in the garbage yesterday. He stood there staring at it. It was easy to see that it was the same one because it had the same jagged chunk cut out of the top lip of its mouth.

At first it took him by surprise, but then he felt annoyed. Not only had someone trespassed on his property to play the same unwanted joke on him, but they'd been in his rubbish bin to retrieve the same pumpkin. That meant that whoever had done this must have seen him put it in there yesterday, which meant that they were probably still watching him now.

Well, if they were watching he'd show them exactly what he thought of their joke AND their trespassing.

Gerald strode back to the garage to retrieve his small axe. He usually only used it for lopping small branches from the two trees in his yard. But he was sure it would be just as useful on a pumpkin.

All his tools were hung neatly on a wooden board on his garage wall. He removed the small axe from the two hooks that were holding it in place and picked up his thick gardening gloves from the workbench under the tool board.

He marched back purposefully to the front porch, looking straight ahead the whole time, even though he was dying to look around and see if anyone was watching him.

He stopped, put down his axe and put on his gloves, not wanting to touch the pumpkin itself. He held it out in front of him as far as his arms could reach and set it down in the middle of the lawn. He retrieved the small, keen-edged axe from the porch and, with repeated blows on the pumpkin, reduced it to small pieces with the face unrecognisable.

He then brought over the wheelie bin, threw the pieces of pumpkin in, and wheeled it back again, feeling satisfied that there was no way anyone could salvage it again.

But he still couldn't understand why someone was doing this to him in the first place. Anyone who knew him would know that he wouldn't appreciate the joke they were trying to play on him. They all knew how much he guarded his privacy and didn't like people trespassing on his property. And not just when it was Halloween, but always. The fences and gates all around his property should be symbolically enough to show that he wanted to keep people out.

And yet despite all this, someone thought it was amusing to gift a Jackolantern to a Halloween-hating, privacy-protective person.

Gerald wanted to know who it was. As soon as he cleaned his axe, he went inside to check his security recordings to see who'd left the pumpkin.

He went straight to his study, opened his laptop computer and opened his security recordings. Usually, the app on his phone would let him know if there was an intruder in the garden because the cameras had motion sensors.

He took his phone out of his back pocket and checked the app. Nothing. There'd been no alerts. Not today or the day before. Without an alert he had no idea what time they brought the pumpkin.

He figured he'd backtrack the recording to midday, thinking that whoever did it needed time to carve it before they delivered it, so had probably left it later in the day.

On the screen there were six small windows, each one displaying what each of the six security cameras could currently see. There was a camera on the front porch, one at each end of the front of the house, one on the back patio, and one at each end of the back of the house.

He clicked on the window for the front porch camera and it opened in a larger window.

At the bottom of the screen was a white line indicating the time over the current 24-hour period starting from midnight. There was a white dot about three-quarters of the way along the line, indicating the current time, which was almost 6 pm. Each of the 24 hours was displayed in a row above the white line. Below it was the previous 2 weeks' recordings, the oldest of which was automatically deleted whenever the current one was saved once the time clicked over to midnight.

Gerald clicked on the dot on the white timeline and dragged it back to just after noon. The image on the screen jumped back to that time.

Gerald was surprised to see the pumpkin was already there. The security camera was in the back corner of the porch, and the angle showed most of the porch, the two steps up to it, and a bit of the front lawn as well.

There was the date and a digital clock in the top-right corner of the window which showed it was 12.06pm.

Gerald backtracked it again to 10 am and then to 8 am, and both times, the pumpkin was already there, He took it back another half hour to 7.30 am when he left for work.

Shocked, he sat back in his chair and stared at the screen. The pumpkin was already there. He was in disbelief. The pumpkin couldn't have already been there or he'd have seen it, wouldn't he? He was sure he'd looked at the porch as he'd left, but now he was doubting himself. He tried to remember reversing out of the garage that morning. What had he been thinking about? Where had he looked as he reversed the car slowly backwards, waiting for the driveway gate to fully open? He was sure he'd scanned the porch briefly, but if he had, how had he not seen the pumpkin?

One thing he was sure about was that the camera never lied. But how did he not see it? It was right at the front of the porch at the top of the steps.

The whole situation seemed weird. It was bad enough thinking that someone was sneaking around his garden and rummaging in his bin while he was at work, but now it looked like they were sneaking around at night when he was asleep.

He sat forward again, desperate to find out when the pumpkin had been left there.

He backtracked 2 hours to 5.30 am. It was already daylight, and the pumpkin was already there. He went back another 2 hours to 3.30 am.

It was still dark, but there was a streetlight right outside Gerald's house, making it easy to see that the pumpkin was gone, or should he rightly say, the pumpkin hadn't arrived yet.

Clearly whoever put the pumpkin there had done it under the cover of darkness, just before the sun started to rise. October is the middle of spring, and the sun was rising much earlier. In a few weeks it would be coming light as early as 3.30am, but for now it was still dark at that time. The pumpkin-putter must have known this and placed the pumpkin on the porch just before it started to get light.

Gerald clicked on "10X" to play the recording forward 10 times faster than normal. Within seconds, the pumpkin appeared. He stopped it playing, confused by what he saw, or more correctly, what he didn't see. No one approached the porch or walked away. The pumpkin just looked as though it appeared by magic. But that couldn't be. The time on the screen read 3.50 am.

He checked the recordings from the two cameras on the front corners of the house. He backtracked the first one to 3.30 am, then played it forward at double speed to 3.50, all the while staring closely to see if he could see someone or see anything, even if it was just a shadow crossing the lawn. The camera was angled to mostly show the driveway, so the porch and most of the front yard weren't visible. But maybe he'd see something. He saw nothing.

He tried the same thing with the other camera which was on the other corner of the house and showed most of the lawn and the front fence and front gate. The porch steps could be seen, but not the porch itself which was recessed. But he didn't see anything or anyone on the recording. So how did the pumpkin get there?

He went back to the porch camera again. He backtracked it to 3.30 am again. No pumpkin. He played it forward in real-time while staring closely at the screen. Everything in the recording was so unmoving it could have been a still image. He watched every part of it. He watched the porch, the lawn, and the steps, but the only thing that moved was the time in the corner of the recording that was counting the minutes.

Gerald kept his face close to the screen, not daring to take his eyes off it for even a second in case he missed something. Nothing moved. Nothing changed. There was no pumpkin. Then suddenly it was there.

"No way," Gerald muttered to himself. He must have missed something. The pumpkin couldn't appear on its own. Someone MUST have put it there.

He moved the recording back to just a few frames before the pumpkin appeared, staring hard as he did so, looking for anything, any small thing that would explain the magically appearing Pumpkin.

But there was nothing. Just the sudden image with the pumpkin in it, and the date and time in the top corner. He was confused. A pumpkin can't just appear like that. He had to be missing something. But what? Whatever it was it had to be at the exact time the pumpkin appeared because there was nothing before it, at least nothing that he had seen.

He moved it back one frame. The pumpkin vanished. He moved it forward one frame. The pumpkin appeared. Exactly 3.50am and there it was. So, what was different about 3.50 and 3.49 and 59 seconds. He flipped the frames back and forth a couple more times. Now you see it. Now you don't. Now you see it now you don't.

But he did see it. He'd missed it before, but now he saw it. In the frame where the pumpkin appeared it was 3.50 am. In the previous frame it was 3.40 am.

A whole 10 minutes was missing. "No way," he muttered to himself again.

He quickly checked the other two camera recordings, and it was the same. 10 minutes missing from 3.40 am to 3.50 am. It was usually a relief when he figured something out, but this raised even more questions.

Somehow the live recordings had been paused for 10 minutes while the pumpkin was taken out of the bin and placed on the porch. It was possible to pause live recordings, but who would do that? And how could they have done it? It seemed impossible that someone could have come into his house (unseen by any cameras), paused the security recordings, gone back outside, taken the pumpkin out of his bin, put it on the porch, gone back inside to restart the recordings, then left unseen. And if they had gone to all that trouble, it was damn creepy. But they couldn't have. No one could have gotten inside his house.

Not only that, But Gerald accessed his cameras from his cell phone and his laptop. His cell phone was with him all night and his laptop was password protected. So how could anyone do it?

What if they had gotten into the house through the back somehow? He got up quickly and checked every door and window, looking for signs of tampering and making sure they were all locked. Nothing seemed like it had been touched or even if it had, there were security screens on every window and security screen doors front and back, so he knew his house was always secure.

He went back to his computer and checked the recordings from the three cameras at the back of the house.

There was nothing unusual on any of them and the time didn't jump forward 10 minutes at 3.40 am. So, whatever was going on it was happening out the front. But what was it? What the hell was going on?

He sat back, his mind almost audibly buzzing with all this new information, which didn't make any sense at all.

Then a thought struck him. Whoever had put the pumpkin there must be the same person who'd put it there the night before.

He checked the recording from the previous day, starting at the time he left for work.

There it was again. The pumpkin was already on the porch. He quickly backtracked to 3.50 am. Just like last night the pumpkin seemed to appear on the porch by magic.

In the previous frame it wasn't there. In the next frame, viola! It appears from nowhere.

He watched it closely again, backtracking a few minutes to see if there was any movement or any clues at all, but there was nothing. Not even a shadow.

He crept it frame by frame to exactly 3.50 am. But then he saw something different. The time didn't jump 10 minutes. It jumped an hour. A whole hour, from 2.50 to 3.50. What were they doing in his garden for an hour? Were they carving the damn thing?

As soon as he thought that he wondered if it was true. "No way," he said to himself once again. The whole thing suddenly felt creepier than before. If they weren't carving the pumpkin, what were they doing? And why?

Maybe he should call the police. And say what? It was a weird story, too weird to try and explain it to someone else. And apart from the obvious trespassing, had the pumpkin person actually committed a crime?

One clear thing was that Gerald was being targeted. Someone (some people?) was sneaking around in his yard at night and somehow getting into his house. He'd never felt so unsafe in his own house before.

His mind went back to the missing hour, and he still wondered what they were doing. The whole thing about them creeping around while he was sleeping scared him. But what could he do about it? There was no one he could talk to, not even the police. What could anyone do about it even if he told them?

Gerald was frightened. He got up and went around the house, checking that all the doors and windows were locked and closing all the curtains. He noticed that it still wasn't completely dark outside yet. The sun had set beyond the horizon, but it was still mostly light outside. The fading light was his opportunity to do what he knew he needed to do to satisfy his curiosity about the missing hour. He needed to go outside and take a look in the wheelie bin.

If they had been carving the pumpkin in his front yard, its innards might be in the bin. He felt slightly foolish for even thinking of it, but he had to know. The only pumpkin pieces he expected to find were the smashed pieces he threw in there earlier, but he still needed to check anyway. What was happening to him was the strangest thing he'd ever come across in his whole life, so he needed to check every possibility, no matter how unlikely. The intruders must have been doing something during the missing hour, after all, they'd paused the recording for an hour for a reason, and he wanted to know why.

Gerald picked up his cell phone and went outside. He turned on the porch light and then hesitated. Now that he was doing it, the possibility of finding the stringy innards and seeds of the pumpkin was worrying. What if they were there? Finding them would make him feel more afraid. No matter whether he found the innards in the bin or not, there was no upside, but he had to find out anyway.

He went down the steps and strode across in front of the house to the bins. He switched on the torch app on his phone, lifted the lid of the general waste bin and peered inside. Just as he did so a chorus of crickets began nearby making him jump. It sounded like they were warning him not to do it. Their shrieking became louder as more crickets joined the chorus. Gerald told himself not to be so paranoid. They were just insects, and they were always noisy at this time of day on warm nights.

He pointed his torchlight into the bin and looked inside. There were two neatly tied bags of rubbish inside. One was the bag of kitchen rubbish that he'd thrown in the night before. The other bag underneath it was a larger bag of pieces of polystyrene and other pieces of packaging that had been in a box in the garage, and he'd decided to get rid of them. The box and packaging were from the new office chair he'd bought for his study a few weeks ago. He always kept all the packaging of new purchases in case he had to return them. But after a few weeks, the chair seemed okay and was extremely comfortable to sit in, so at the weekend he decided it was time to get rid of the box and everything in it, which included a large bag that easily fit all the polystyrene packaging.

On top of the two bags were all the pumpkin pieces he'd thrown in.

Gerald felt momentarily relieved. But then a thought struck him.

The previous evening, he'd thrown the bag of kitchen rubbish in the bin, assuming that it must have landed on top of the pumpkin that he'd dropped in there earlier. But neither when he'd dropped the pumpkin in there, nor later when he'd thrown the bag in, had he thought to look inside the bin. So, the bag of kitchen waste might have landed on top of the other bag if the pumpkin had already been removed. But the security recording only showed a 10-minute jump in time at 3.40 am, which was, presumably, when someone removed the pumpkin from the bin and put it back on the porch. So he must have dropped the pumpkin on top of all the carved-out flesh.

He opened the lid fully, letting it swing down and clunk against the back of the bin. With the torch still in his other hand, he slowly reached into the bin, trying not to touch the smashed pumpkin pieces with his bare hand and lifted the corner of the kitchen bag.

Some of the smashed pieces tumbled further into the bin and some rolled and touched his hand. He grimaced but still hung onto the edge of the bag because he had to know what was underneath.

He pulled the plastic higher and pushed the bag to one side. There underneath it was the stringy flesh and seeds from the pumpkin, along with the cut outs from the carved face, sitting on top of the other rubbish bag.

Gerald was so surprised his hand flew off the bag as though he'd had an electric shock.

As fast as he could, he swung the lid back over and closed the bin, turned off his torch app, and headed back inside as fast as he could, trying not to show the absolute panic he was feeling.

He couldn't wait to get back inside. He closed the front door, locked it, and leaned against it. He needed to get his jumbled thoughts together.

Finding the pumpkin flesh in the bin raised even more questions and none of it was making sense.

Whoever it was, why did they carve the pumpkin at his house? Surely if they'd wanted to leave a Jackolantern as a prank, they'd carve it at their own house first, not come over here, stop the recordings, go back outside, carve the pumpkin, put it on the porch, throw the carved-out flesh in the bin and then come back inside to start the recordings again and not be seen. And why were they doing any of this anyway?

What the hell was going on?

The answer must be in the recordings somewhere because there was no way they could come and go unseen without leaving a clue anywhere. He just needed to go through the recordings a few more times until he could see what was missing.

But first he wanted to shower and have dinner. He needed to do something normal because everything had been so weird and abnormal since he came home.

He headed to the bathroom, confident that after a shower and a meal, he'd be able to sit down and watch the security recordings, frame-by-frame if he had to, and he'd find the answer hidden in there somewhere. He just knew it.

Dreaming

Gerald woke with a fright, his heart pounding crazily in his chest. He checked the time on his phone. It was 3.40 am.

He'd been dreaming about the pumpkin being back on the porch. The dream seemed so real. He'd dreamt that he woke up in the early hours of the morning, opened the front door, and there was the pumpkin, perfectly pieced back together.

He got such a fright in his dream that it woke him. Now he lay there wondering if the dream was a premonition or if his subconscious knew that the pumpkin was back. It wasn't lost on him that he'd woken up at the same time the pumpkin had previously appeared. Did his mind know it was pumpkin time? Had the pumpkin woken him up when it arrived? Was it sitting on the porch pieced back together just like it was in his dream?

Logic told him that none of that could happen. No one would go to so much trouble to get all the broken pieces out of his bin, even those that had fallen into the bottom, and glue them all back together just to play a trick on him. He lay there in the dark fighting the urge to go and have a look on the porch.

He reached over and picked up his phone. He checked the app for his security cameras. Nothing. The porch was empty, and there was no sign of movement outside, yet somehow it didn't make him feel any easier.

He closed the app, darkened the screen and put the phone down. He wondered that if he were to check the app again, would the pumpkin be there? Or was someone out there right now piecing it together?

Damn it! Now that he was awake, he needed to pee.

He threw back the covers, got out of bed and headed down the hallway to the bathroom without putting any lights on. He'd made the trip from bed to bathroom so many times he could probably do it with his eyes closed, which was fortunate because right now he was reluctant to put a light on.

No one in the whole world knew that he was up and he wanted to keep it that way. If someone was out there, they wouldn't know where he was, which made a change because they must be always watching him.

Once he'd been to the bathroom, he went back into the bedroom and stopped. He wanted to check the front porch. He was up anyway and wide awake, and no one else knew it, so if there was someone outside, they'd get a fright when he opened the door. It was still dark outside but there was always enough light from the streetlights to see anyone if they were out there, and it was also all the light he needed to give him a little bit more bravado.

He went to the front door and put his ear against it to see if he could hear anything first. Nothing except a few distant birds welcoming the new day.

He stood up, took a deep breath, and yanked the door open, bracing himself for whoever or whatever might be out there.

Nothing but silence on the porch. No pumpkin. No person. Just silence. Gerald wasn't sure how to feel about that. If the pumpkin had been there, it would have unnerved him. Not seeing it unnerved him even more. Was it not there because he'd smashed it to pieces?

Or was it because the person hadn't finished gluing it back together yet? Either way, he was scared. His dream had frightened him and now he was shaking. This whole pumpkin prank was distressing. He needed to close the door to feel safe again.

He craned his neck slightly forward to check the garden was free of strangers as he slowly closed the door, intending to disappear safely behind it and get on with his day. There was no way he could go back to sleep now, but he'd be able to go to work early and get plenty of work done in peace before the rest of his colleagues started arriving for the day.

But as he pushed the door closed, he looked up and that's when he saw it. He'd been so intent on making sure there was no one on his property that he hadn't noticed what was outside of it, on the street.

His door-closing arm froze and he let out an involuntary sound that went "Ugh!"

Standing on the road outside his gate, was a man with a Jackolantern for a head. And the pumpkin face was staring straight at him.

The Pumpkin Man

Gerald didn't want to see the pumpkin man and didn't want to accept what he was seeing because it couldn't be real, but he couldn't stop staring at it. He couldn't pull his gaze away.

Who was it? Why were they there? What were they going to do? How did they know Gerald was awake?

The pumpkin man stood motionless. As Gerald stared at him, he realised that the Jackolantern wasn't a replacement for his head, it was over his head. But how could that be? How could anyone fit their head inside a pumpkin? Yet there he was. The pumpkin was probably no bigger than a man's head anyway, so how did his head fit inside it?

The pumpkin man stood there, hands by his sides, staring at Gerald the whole time. He was tall with a slim build, but Gerald hardly noticed because he couldn't stop staring at the pumpkin head. It was the one he'd chopped up and put in the bin. It had been repaired somewhat raggedly, but the crudely missing chunk on the side of its mouth was still visible.

Somehow, and Gerald wasn't sure if it was his imagination or not, the pumpkin face looked angry, as though it was annoyed with him for cutting it up.

The pumpkin man still didn't move, and Gerald continued to stare, slowly taking notice of the rest of the pumpkin man.

The tall, slim body was wearing a red checked shirt, a blue sleeveless body warmer, and a pair of blue jeans.

Now Gerald's full attention was on these clothes. He'd seen them before. It was the clothes that his friend Roger was wearing when he died. And just like the pumpkin man, Roger was tall and slim, the opposite of short, stocky Gerald.

Roger was the reason Gerald had moved away from Mount Eden.

On the day that he died, Roger had asked Gerald to go for a walk with him up one of the mountains near where they lived. Gerald hated walking and hated heights, which was why he'd never walked up any of the mountains, even though all the locals did.

All the local mountains were said to be made out of volcanic rock and were thousands of years old.

Some of the tracks were known to be dangerous and sometimes there were rock falls even while people were walking on them. Several times a year hikers had to be rescued from the mountains if they got caught in bad weather or they went off one of the tracks and got lost or the path broke away while they were on it.

Gerald always wondered why people still wanted to hike up the mountains when it was so dangerous.

Till one day ten years ago when Roger, who was an avid hiker, begged Gerald to go with him. Against his better judgment, Gerald went. Halfway up the mountain, Roger slipped when the edge of the path they were on suddenly cracked, and a large chunk of it fell away. He remembered hearing it smash and break into pieces as it rolled down the mountainside.

Roger was walking near the edge of the path when it cracked right under his foot. It broke away instantly taking Roger with it.

At first Roger only slipped but was unable to keep his balance because of the moving ground under his feet. He pinwheeled his arms and moved his feet so fast that he looked like he was tap dancing. He shouted, "Gerald! Help!" But Gerald did nothing. He stood and watched his friend struggle for only a few seconds before he disappeared over the side of the mountain to his death.

Gerald had continued to stand there for quite a while afterwards not knowing what to do. Should he go for help or was it too late?

He stood there feeling guilty for not helping his friend. He stood there a long time. Eventually, his mind raced forward into the future as he ran through different scenarios of what would happen next. Would he be blamed for pushing him? When Roger's body was found, could he act innocent as though he knew nothing about it? No one knew that he'd gone up the mountain, and he'd never been up before, so no one would even guess that he'd been here with Roger.

So, he said nothing. But Roger's disappearance was big news in a small town like Mount Eden, and people talked about it all the time.

Everyone hoped Roger was alive and well somewhere, but as days turned into weeks, turned into months, it became apparent that Roger was never coming back, but that didn't stop people talking about it constantly.

After a year, Gerald left Mount Eden and moved to the city.

That was 9 years ago. During that time Gerald learned to live with his guilt. He'd always felt that no one here knew about Roger, but clearly they did, because here was the pumpkin man dressed like Roger.

Gerald's fear of the pumpkin man suddenly overwhelmed him, and with shaking hands, he slammed the front door and locked it.

What the hell was going on? The mystery of the pumpkin was getting deeper and deeper. And it had happened in only 3 days. 3 days of mental torture for Gerald.

His immediate fear was where was the pumpkin man now? Was he still on the street or was he, God forbid, in the garden now or on the porch?

Maybe, and this was his hope, the pumpkin man hadn't been there at all. Maybe he just dreamed it, just like he dreamed about the pumpkin being on the porch and then he woke up. If there was any mercy for him, he'd wake up now.

But it wasn't a dream, and he wasn't about to wake up. He knew that. He just wanted to make it all stop. To make it not real. He wanted to know why all this was happening to him.

At first he'd thought it was a neighbour playing a Halloween prank on him, but now he knew it couldn't be because none of them knew about Roger. And the pumpkin man couldn't be real. He just couldn't.

Then another thought struck him. What if the pumpkin man was Roger? Roger was the only person who knew that Gerald was with him on the mountain that day. Maybe he'd come back for revenge for not helping him.

But Roger was dead. He saw him fall, and he heard him fall. If he was alive, he'd have let his family know. He wouldn't have run away and stayed hidden all these years.

But if it wasn't Roger, then who was the pumpkin man and why was he dressed in Roger's clothes?

Damn it! Why did nothing make sense anymore?

But sense or not, the pumpkin man was real. He was out there standing on the street. Or was he?

Gerald went to the front living room windows, pulled aside the curtain with his trembling hand and peered out, half expecting to see the pumpkin man outside his window staring straight back at him.

But he wasn't there, not on the porch and not in the street. Not seeing him was more frightening than seeing him because now Gerald didn't know where he was, and that terrified him.

Why was this happening? And who was the pumpkin man?

It was only three days ago that he thought it was a neighbour playing a simple prank. Then he was annoyed that they'd taken the pumpkin back out of his bin, which annoyed him. And they'd somehow got into the house and paused the security camera recordings without being seen, which seemed impossible.

And now they had pieced the big pumpkin back together and worn it on their head and somehow knew he was up early and had stood outside his gate waiting for him.

Who the hell would do such a thing? And why?

The other thing now though, was the clothes. Why was the pumpkin man wearing the exact clothes that Roger died in, right down to his expensive white trainers? Roger's clothes on the pumpkin man bothered him a lot.

Did someone know what happened?

Is that what all this was about?

Roger That

Gerald had met Roger way back in primary school when Roger and his family had moved to Mount Eden. The two boys were polar opposites in every way, yet the two of them instantly liked each other and bonded together immediately.

Gerald admired Roger's outgoing personality and confidence, and Roger liked Gerald's quiet manner. But it wasn't just their personalities that were different. Gerald had always had a thick-set build, while Roger was slim and athletic. Gerald had a fascination with computers and software, while Roger was always engaged in different sports. When they were older Gerald became a computer coder and Roger became a builder. The two of them remained close friends the whole time.

Gerald believed that even though they were so different from each other, the one thing they had in common was intelligence. When they were kids, all the other boys were busy acting stupid and making fun of each other. Gerald was an avid reader and was always reading. When he wasn't reading, he was learning about computers and how they worked. At the same time, Roger was busy with sports and was always playing on one team or another at the weekends. When he wasn't doing that he was busy with other physical activities like swimming, running, and hiking up the local mountains, or he was helping his father with DIY jobs around their own house or doing jobs for other people.

As teenagers, while the other guys were all chasing girls and bragging to each other about their conquests (both real and imagined), Gerald and roger were still progressing towards their ultimate careers, which seemed to attract girls to them, so they were enjoying their youth, and probably more than the other boys.

Eventually, Gerald got a job with a software company where he quickly became a valued employee. Because of his love of what he was doing, his knowledge, speed and quality of his work were far superior to the other employees. He enjoyed his job, and unlike most people, he looked forward to going to work every day. When he wasn't at work doing coding, he was at home reading articles, books, and magazines to learn more and keep up with all the advances in the computer and software industry.

At the same time, Roger became an apprentice builder. A few years later, at age 24, he set up his own company. Just like Gerald, Roger loved what he did, so he was good at it, and had so many clients that he constantly had to turn down work.

Life was good for both Gerald and Roger. They were both dating, adored their girlfriends, and were doing well in their jobs. Gerald had received a promotion and was earning good money, far more than most young men his age.

But a year later, Roger disappeared. Gerald would never forget that day. It was a day that changed his life forever.

He'd been at home that afternoon studying some new software and how it worked so that he could improve it. His parents and sisters were out, so he had the peace of the whole house to himself. He was sitting out on the back patio working on his computer when he heard the side gate open and close, and Roger appeared from around the corner of the house.

"Hey, what you doing cramped up back here on such a glorious day," said Roger.

He was right about the weather. There had been three days that week of heavy downpours, but the weekend had been warm and sunny. It was Sunday afternoon, and the neighbourhood was quiet because most people were out enjoying the nice weather.

It was the end of October, Spring, a cool time of year before summer hit in December.

Right now, in Spring, it was warm, but not too warm yet to go out. Gerald was never bothered about going out anywhere, but he did appreciate being able to sit outside, even if flies and small spiders kept sitting on his fingers on the keyboard.

He said to Roger, "How did you know I was here?"

"I didn't. I knocked but no one answered so I came to see if anyone was out back. Surely you're not working."

"Just studying some new stuff."

"How about taking a break and coming with me? I haven't seen you much lately."

"Come with you where?"

"A trek up the mountains."

"All of them?"

"Ha ha, no. Just one will do."

Gerald had never before hiked up any of the local mountains. They weren't high but they were steep. "You know I don't like walking if I have nowhere to go. It's pointless."

"Oh, come on. I haven't seen you lately so we can catch up."

"We can stay here and do that."

Aww, please? I was going to walk on my own, but it will be more fun with the two of us."

Gerald sighed. "You know I don't like hiking up the mountains."

Roger laughed. "You've never tried. You might love it."

Gerald knew he'd hate it. He didn't have to try something to know he wouldn't like it. And he'd never made any secret of his dislike of walking up mountain trails. He always bragged that he'd never done it and never would.

Roger continued with his persuasion. "We can go to the smallest one."

"Isn't that the steepest one?"

"Well…. Yeah…. But it's only a short trail, and it's not steep the whole way. Aww, come on."

"Okay, I guess it won't hurt just this once." Gerald surprised himself with his own words. But he hadn't seen Roger for a couple of weeks, and it would be great to hang out with him. "We can take my car."

"Good, because I didn't bring mine."

"How were you going to get to the mountain?"

"Walk, of course."

Gerald was not surprised at Roger's plan to walk to a mountain before hiking to the top of it. Roger seemed to have no limits when it came to physical activity. He just loved being outside doing stuff.

Gerald put away his computer, and they drove to Mount Little. All the locals called it that. It did have an official name, but Gerald could never remember it because it was spelled in a strange way with only two vowels but many consonants, so it was more like a sound than a word. That's why everyone simply called it Mount Little, and even papers and brochures written about the area referenced it by its nickname.

Gerald put on the best walking shoes he had but wasn't sure if they'd be suitable. All of his footwear had been purchased for the sole purpose of street walking or indoor walking, like his office shoes. Never had he thought that he might need them for walking up a mountain.

Right from the start Gerald thought Mount Little was too steep to walk up, but Roger reassured him that it wasn't. "This is nothing," he said with a big smile as they started up the mountain. "It will get worse, but not for long." Gerald failed to see how telling him that the path would get worse was reassuring.

The path quickly became much steeper and then so steep that Gerald could put his hand out to touch the path in front of him. He was almost out of breath and felt a drip if sweat trickle down one side of his face.

Roger, on the other hand, was still chatting and bounding around like a puppy, jumping up to hit small tree branches and running his outstretched hand along tall grasses. It was as if he couldn't tell how severe the incline was. But how could he not know?

Gerald stopped, bent over, and placed his palms on his thighs. He breathed in a couple of deep lungs full of air, then stood up and wiped his hands all over his face to remove the sweat. He carefully looked behind him. The path was so steep it almost looked like a drop.

He knew it would be a lot harder walking back down than it was walking up. His leg muscles ached, and his breathing was heavy. Surely no one in their right mind could think this was fun, yet there was Roger, only slightly out of breath, still smiling, and asking, "You, okay?"

Gerald took a couple more breaths and said, "How much further are we going?" He felt so hot. He knew that the day was only warm, but right now he could feel his face burning deep red and sweat covered every inch of his body. His shorts and T-shirt, which previously felt light and cool, now felt thick and way too heavy for this heat. He was thankful for all the trees shading them from the sun.

Roger tapped him on his upper arm and said, "Come on, it's not much further."

"What's not much further?" puffed Gerald.

"There's an amazing view up ahead. There's a parting in the trees and you can see for miles"

"I'm whacked."

"It's not far. Just a few more steps." Roger started walking and shouted, "Come on, or you'll have to run to catch me up."

Gerald, having no choice but to keep going, followed him. The path was stoney with patches of grass and weeds dotted around and it curved the whole way, so it was impossible to see too far ahead. Gerald hoped that the parting in the trees would come into view soon because he didn't know how much more of this torture he could take. It was exhausting carrying his heavy body up a mountain. He wasn't thin and physically fit like Roger.

"There it is," announced Roger, pointing ahead. Gerald could see that there was indeed a noticeable gap in the trees at the cliff side of the path. He just hoped Roger didn't expect him to stand close to the edge. Heights scared him, especially if there was no safety railing.

Roger jogged ahead. How the hell he had the energy to go faster, Gerald had no idea. Roger got to the tree gap and stepped forward, closer to the edge and called back, "Be careful when you get here. It looks like there's been a bit of a landslide here."

Gerald wasn't interested. All he wanted to do was catch up with Roger, look at the view, then get the hell back down the mountain without losing his balance and breaking a leg.

The path was wider at the gap in the trees, probably because so many people had stood there over the years. The path was just a well-worn track from thousands of people walking over it every year, and the wider part of it at the gap was an extension of that.

"It's loose here," said Roger looking down at his feet. Where he was standing the ground was cracked. It looked like quite a deep fissure, and it was only a few inches from the edge, which from where Gerald was standing, looked like a sheer drop. "Shouldn't you be careful?"

Roger scuffed his feet back and forth a few times over the wide crack. "It looks like there's been a bit of a breakaway here, but I don't think it will get any wider. It's all the loose stones here that are a bit slippery. It's like walking on marbles."

That was the last solid memory Gerald had of their time on the mountain.

Just as Roger finished speaking, the split second he finished as Gerald remembered, the crack that Roger said wouldn't get any wider, did.

A strange, deep popping sound came from under Roger's feet. Both men looked at each other, then looked down at the ground, just as the crack in the dirt widened and one side of the path fell away and disappeared over the edge.

Roger, who'd had one foot on the ground that fell away began to lose his balance.

Before the ground fell away, he was close to the edge. Now he was teetering on it, a look of fear and disbelief on his face.

To Gerald, it all seemed to be happening in slow motion, yet at the same time, it all happened so fast that his mind was unable to comprehend what was happening as it was happening.

Roger desperately tried to regain his balance, but there was no longer anything stable under his feet. He attempted to turn on one foot and move back to the safety of solid ground but fell forward as he slid on the loose ground. The more he tried to stand up, the more he slid backwards. There were too many stones under his feet.

Roger slid backwards over the rocky edge, trying to grab hold of anything he could to stop himself from falling, but there was not much to hang onto. He grasped one clump of long grass and then another, but both were uprooted.

Gerald stood frozen, watching his friend fight for his life. When Roger called out to him for help, he briefly thought of stepping forward to try and help, but the thought was only fleeting. What if Roger pulled him over the edge too? And then Roger was gone.

Things were happening so fast, yet the horror of it all was happening so slowly. Gerald heard Roger bouncing off the rock face of the mountain. The sound echoed all around. There were large outcropping rocks all over the side of the mountain, and it sounded like Roger was hitting them all. At the same time, Gerald could hear what sounded like breaking bones.

Then the noises stopped, and there was an eerie silence. No birds. No wind. Just silence and everything seemed unnaturally still.

Gerald stood there for a long time, stunned, unable to comprehend what he had just seen. It didn't seem real. He didn't know what to do, so he just stood there.

After a while, he heard a bird start calling. It was a crow. Then another one answered. Other birds began to join in until all the sounds on the mountain were back to normal. Or had they stopped at all? Gerald was unsure of anything. It all seemed so surreal, so dreamlike.

He stepped forward slowly and carefully, standing as close to the edge as he dared. He stared hard at his feet, watching for the slightest hint of slippage or any more ground breaking away. The ground seemed firm, but he still didn't trust it. To be safe, he laid down to spread his weight, snaking forward enough to be able to peer down over the edge.

As he inched his way forward, something white caught his eye. He turned and saw a rock half sticking out of the ground that had been painted white. It had a bit of an iceberg look to it, as though it was the tip of a much larger rock underground. But why had someone come up here with some white paint just to paint that rock? An even bigger question was, why was he even thinking about that right now?

Gerald reached the edge, small stones falling all around him as he looked down.

He was glad he wasn't standing up because being this high up made him feel dizzy.

There was nothing but large rocks sticking out of the mountainside all the way down. No wonder Roger had hit so many. At the bottom, there were trees, boulders and what looked like other assorted plants and huge ferns. There were also a few trees growing between the rocks on the side of the mountain, and there, hanging in a fork of one of them was Roger.

Gerald took a sharp intake of breath. Until now it was hard to believe what had happened was real, but now he could see Roger's lifeless body, dressed in his red-checked shirt, blue body warmer, and blue jeans.

He stared for what seemed like a long time, perhaps waiting to see if Roger moved or showed any sign of life, perhaps not. He didn't know what he was thinking or feeling anymore.

He sat up cross-legged and tried to think as he wiped the dirt off his clothes. Part of what he was feeling was guilt because he hadn't done anything to help his friend. But worrying about it wouldn't help. He needed to do something now, but it felt wrong to walk away and leave Roger hanging there.

He took out his phone, thinking that he should call someone. But who? And what would he say? And would he be blamed for what happened? He stared at his phone. It seemed so weird after what had happened that he was looking at something so normal right now. Looking at the phone he could see that it was out of range up here. He put his phone back in his pocket.

He leaned over and looked at Roger hanging in the tree by his armpits and staring straight back up at him. Gerald got up and made his way back down the mountain. It was too steep to hurry and going down was much more painful on his leg muscles than walking up. He had no idea what he was going to do. He just needed to leave.

He got in his car and drove straight home. The rest of his family still wasn't there. He got his computer out and sat outside at the patio table right where he'd been when Roger had arrived. He wished that being back there meant that nothing had happened. He wished he'd been there the whole time.

He was still sweating from his walk back down the mountain. The thoughts in his mind were jumbled, unable to think of anything.

Then he heard a noise he recognised. Voices. The rest of his family had arrived.

"We're home," his mother called out merrily. Gerald went inside, terrified that they'd know something was wrong and ask him about it.

His parents and two sisters were all in the kitchen, putting groceries away and chatting together happily.

His father glanced up at him briefly and said, "Put the kettle on will you?"

Gerald complied without speaking. The normality seemed surreal after his horror trip up the mountain and seeing Roger fall to his death. He wanted to tell them, but tell them what? "Hey everyone. I went for a walk up the mountain with Roger, and he fell off a cliff."

"Is he alright?"

"No idea. I left him and got the hell out of there."

How could he tell them any of that?

He couldn't.

Instead, he went outside onto the patio with his family and they all had coffee and cake and chatted happily with no one noticing that Gerald was quieter than his usual self. And although Gerald sat with them, he felt like he was in his own bubble, knowing something terrible had happened, something that no one in the whole world knew about but him. But he knew that soon everyone would know that Roger was gone.

The next day, everyone was talking about Roger. Several people called Gerald to ask if he knew anything, including Roger's mother. Gerald didn't answer any of the calls but did answer their voicemails via text message to say that he was sorry, but he hadn't seen Roger.

He felt the pressure of his guilt for lying coupled with the worry that someone might have seen him with

Roger the day before, but no one did.

For that whole week, he felt like he was living a dream that felt more like a waking nightmare, of going to work, coming home and having to endure listening to people talk about Roger's disappearance. People were talking about nothing else. Many of them even came to the house to talk about it and asked Gerald repeatedly if he knew anything.

Gerald struggled all the time with the guilt of lying, especially to Roger's family who were distraught. He also tried to act as though he too was concerned about Roger, which was the hardest of all. Gerald had always been a quiet and private person and that helped him because no one expected him to say a much anyway.

The police were brought in after the first couple of days and questioned everyone in town regardless of whether they knew Roger or not. But no one knew where Roger had gone that day or who he was with, much to Gerald's relief. He thought that for sure at least one person would have seen him with Roger that day.

The day that the police knocked at the door of Gerald's house, he had the sinking feeling that they'd come to say that they had a witness who'd seen him with Roger. Gerald tensed up for questioning, but they'd only come to ask general questions of everyone. Regardless of that, seeing two police officers in the house fully loaded with tasers, guns, handcuffs and bulletproof vests, felt intimidating, and Gerald remained tense until they left and the door closed behind them.

After the first week of questioning, the police then began organising searches of all the local mountains because that was where Roger often walked alone.

Gerald spent that week much the same as the last. He went to work every day and came home to endure the latest gossip about his missing friend. Only this time, he had the problem of how he would react when they told him that Roger's body had been found hanging in a tree. Could he feign surprise?

He'd done nothing for the past two weeks but think about Roger hanging in that tree, and that it was only a matter of time before someone else saw him there.

But much to Gerald's surprise, the search was called off at the end of the week because nothing had been found. He was shocked as well as puzzled. How had they not found Roger? He was hanging in plain sight, and there'd been what looked like hundreds of rescue crews searching all week using dogs, helicopters and even drones. It had been all over the news on the TV.

When he heard that the search had been called off, he was perplexed. Surely, they would have found him.

Gerald thought about it all weekend. No matter what he was doing his mind kept drifting back to the image of Roger hanging in the tree in full sight of anyone who looked over the edge, yet for some reason, drones, helicopters and dozens of police and search and rescue teams couldn't see him.

Then a thought struck him. What if the reason no one saw him was because he wasn't there? What if Roger was still alive? What if the fall hadn't killed him?

Now his mind raced through several possibilities.

Roger was only knocked unconscious. But Gerald had heard so many bones break,

Roger was injured and had managed to free himself from the tree. So where was he?

Roger was hiding somewhere to teach Gerald a lesson. But why would he put his family through such anguish?

Gerald needed to know if Roger was still in the tree.

He got his car keys and shouted a brief "I'm just going out for a bit," to his parents who were sitting out on the patio, and left.

When he got to the mountain, he began walking up the narrow path, studying the ground as he went, hoping it would be easy to find the exact place where Roger had fallen.

After a while he spotted a familiar object. The white painted rock at the gap in the trees. Next to it was the bite out of the edge of the track that had given way under Roger's feet.

Gerald's heart had already been beating fast because of the exertion from walking uphill. Now it beat faster.

Since leaving this mountain exactly two weeks ago, Gerald could almost convince himself that everything that happened up here was a dream. But now it felt all too real again.

He stood there for a few seconds breathing deeply, looking around to make sure he was alone. Then he got down on his hands and knees and crawled to the edge, small stones digging into his knees and palms as he went, terrified of the ground giving way beneath him, just as it had done to Roger.

He peered over the edge. There was the top of the tree several metres below. Roger was not there.

Gerald stayed there unmoving for a few minutes, looking below the tree for any glimpse of Roger's red checked shirt visible amongst the large ferns and the tangle of thick vines and weeds below. But there was nothing.

The tangle below looked dense enough that nothing could fall through it. But if Roger had fallen, the weight of his body would have broken through it.

Since Roger's fall, there had been mostly hot and sunny weather, but one night there'd been a huge thunderstorm that had woken the whole family in the middle of the night. Maybe the storm had dislodged Roger's body from the fork in the tree. Or had he wriggled out of it himself?

Gerald crawled back to the centre of the path and stood up, brushing the stones and dirt from his knees and palms, and walked back down the mountain. His movements were slow and calm, but his mind was screaming at him that maybe he had left Roger to die. Maybe he could have gotten him some help. But at the time he'd been so sure that Roger was dead. Hadn't he?

For the next few months, he had to endure the constant chatter and guesswork about what had happened to Roger. Even at home, the talk around the dinner table was often, "We were talking about Roger last night at the pub, and someone said that maybe..."

He wasn't safe from the gossip anywhere, and he struggled with the fear that Roger would be found, and it would be hard not to blurt out the truth. Or what if Roger was found alive?

It was almost a year to the day of Roger's disappearance that Gerald moved to Brisbane to get away from all the talk about Roger.

He was fortunate to get the first job he applied for with a tech firm in the city.

They hired him on the spot and asked, "When can you start?"

Gerald quit his job as soon as he got home that day and they let him go almost immediately, which wasn't unusual in his line of work. Tech companies didn't want disgruntled coders to have access to all their systems and servers.

It was hard to say goodbye to all his friends and family and to leave the place where he grew up, but he had to go in case he slipped up and said something he shouldn't. He had to keep his secret, which was especially hard around Roger's parents. He hated to watch them suffer. They'd even said that it would be easier to know that Roger was dead. That was when Gerald felt he couldn't take it any longer, so he took the coward's way out and left.

In the city he was lucky enough to find somewhere to live almost immediately. He'd checked into an apartment hotel for a week, and during that time found a furnished apartment that had been a holiday rental, but the owners wanted to rent it out permanently, which suited Gerald because it was not only furnished but fully equipped and Gerald's meagre possessions were only his clothes and a few personal items.

At work he threw himself into his job. He enjoyed the work and loved having his own office. They were paying him a high salary and expected big things from him which suited Gerald because he loved being given all the big jobs to do.

He immersed himself fully in every project and worked long hours every day so that he didn't have to think about anything else. When he wasn't working, he was studying the latest magazines, books and other publications to keep up with everything to do with coding and computer programming. It was an industry that required constant learning and updating.

It only took a few weeks of total immersion in his new job and life in the city for Gerald to feel far removed from all the Roger talk. It almost felt like none of it happened, except the guilt for not telling anyone still haunted his soul.

Halloween came around again a year after he moved, a dreaded reminder of all that had happened, and it prompted Gerald to move again.

This time he bought a house in the suburbs, only a short drive to work, and had been happy here for eight years, having minimal contact with his family and never returning to Mount Eden.

Every Halloween had been a fresh reminder that Roger was still missing, and his fear that somehow his secret would come out, that someone would remember they saw him on the mountain with Roger.

And now his fear was intensified with the appearance of the pumpkin man wearing the same clothes as Roger when he fell.

The pumpkin man had to be Roger. No one else knew that Gerald was with him when he fell off the mountain. He'd left Roger hanging by his armpits in the tree. Surely he was dead. He'd broken so many bones in the fall. He'd looked dead.

Pumpkin Magic

All his life, Gerald had kept mostly to himself, and he liked it that way. But now after seeing the pumpkin man outside his gate in the early hours of the morning, he wished there was someone with him, someone to see what he had seen and offer ideas about what was going on.

This whole thing had seemed like a simple (although somewhat twisted) prank in the beginning, but now it was a lot more than that.

Somewhere in his mind he was still trying to convince himself that the pumpkin man wasn't Roger. It couldn't be. But how else could he explain the clothes the pumpkin man had been wearing? The same clothes that Roger had been wearing when he fell. That couldn't be a coincidence, could it?

Because of the identical clothing, it couldn't be one of his neighbours playing a practical joke on him. Not only that, why would they?

Gerald didn't particularly like his neighbours, but he didn't dislike them either, and he'd never said or done anything wrong to any of them. He treated his neighbours the same way he treated everyone. Distantly. He much preferred his own company. Even at work he only spoke to others if he needed to and never spent time with them socially, except for a few occasions when he'd had an after-work drink with them at a bar, and even then after one drink he'd left and gone home.

Gerald looked out of the living room window one more time. Nothing on the porch. No one in the street. All was quiet. Too quiet. He turned on the TV. A movie was on. It looked like an old movie from the 70's or 80's. He didn't care what it was as long as there were no pumpkins in it. He sat and watched it just to try and get his mind off the pumpkin man, who had disturbed him more than he would admit to himself. He tried desperately to absorb himself in whatever the banal movie was on the TV, but no matter how much he tried to concentrate, the image of the pumpkin man remained in his head.

The ringing of the alarm on his phone made him jump. He hadn't realised how long he'd been sitting there. He must have fallen asleep.

The TV was still on. It looked like some kind of early-morning news show.

Gerald stood up, stretched and turned off the TV and the alarm. The sound of birds outside filled the interior silence. Daylight was peaking around the edges of the curtains.

He went to open them and momentarily hesitated. He was still frightened from the last time he looked outside. Even the welcoming daylight couldn't diminish all his fears. There still could be the pumpkin on the porch again.

But there was nothing. He threw the curtains open quickly and saw nothing.

Maybe it was all over.

Maybe the pumpkin man was the finale.

It all had to stop sometime and maybe this was it.

Maybe.

Gerald felt tired all day at work. Tired through lack of sleep and tired of whoever was doing all this to him.

He knuckle-dragged his way through the day. Whenever someone came into his office to ask him something, he had to ask them to repeat what they said because he was too tired to understand them the first time, and he struggled to keep his mind on his work. All day the temptation to lay his head on his desk and take a nap was strong. He was glad when it was finally time to go home, and he was looking forward to going to bed early.

When he got home, as he swung the car onto his driveway, he tried to stare straight ahead and not look at the porch. But as he sat in his car, waiting for the garage door to open in front of him and the sliding gate to close behind him, he turned his head and was relieved to see the porch was empty. But his relief was short-lived when he saw the pumpkin in the middle of the lawn halfway between the porch and the pedestrian gate. It was the same glued-together one that the pumpkin man had been wearing, battered, glued back together and looking annoyed. The mouth and eyes were now misshapen into an angry scowl.

All day he'd been anxious, hoping it was all over, yet fearful of what might come next.

Now he felt angry, angrier than the scowl on the pumpkin's face. Enough was enough. How far and for how long was this person going to go to try and scare him?

It was all to do with the pumpkin. The damn pumpkin. He needed to get rid of it once and for all.

Gerald parked the car in the garage and got out, slamming the door shut behind him. He took the small axe from the wall where it hung neatly in place amongst his other tools, picked up his shovel and strode over to the pumpkin. He looked neither left nor right as he went. His eyes were only on the pumpkin. He didn't know if the person who put it there was watching or not, but he hoped they were. A few of his neighbours were outside in their gardens as he drove down the street. Perhaps one of them was the culprit after all. Perhaps not. Either way, he didn't care right now.

He went straight to the pumpkin and rained down blow after blow on it with his axe. Previously it had been hard to cut into, but this time it was slightly easier given the pumpkins' previous injuries.

He brought the axe down on it again and again until it was in many more pieces than it was before.

By the time he finished he was exhausted, chest heaving with deep breaths. He was sweating too, and not because it was a warm spring evening.

He stood and stared down at the pile of orange pieces while he waited for his heavy breathing to subside. Despite his anger at the pumpkin, he was afraid to touch it, but he had to get rid of it, get it out of sight.

He shoveled it up using the axe to push the pieces onto the shovel, took it to the bin and dropped it in. It took three goes to pick up all the pieces. All that was left was a patch of orange sludge that Gerald wiped into the grass with his shoe.

Even though he'd never looked up the whole time, he could feel people watching him. No doubt they thought he was crazy, but he didn't care. They were his neighbours, not his friends. He took his axe and shovel back to the garage to clean them, letting the electric door close behind him.

As soon as he'd finished cleaning them and put them away, he went straight to his study and took out his laptop computer. He backtracked the security recordings looking for the time the pumpkin had been placed on his lawn. He backtracked to mid-morning and, just like the other times, the pumpkin seemed to appear by magic.

He slowed down and watched it frame by frame, but it was the same as before. Now you see it, now you don't (or the reverse of that), and 10 minutes were missing. He watched it several times, frame by frame, face close to the screen, looking for something, anything, to see if there was someone there, someone entering the front yard before the time jump. But there was nothing.

His anger began to dissipate and was slowly replaced by fear. Why was someone doing this to him? The whole damn thing was creepy with someone watching him, and when he wasn't there, coming into his yard and gluing pumpkin pieces back together. And the biggest mystery of all was how they were pausing his security recordings AND without being seen.

And what about the pumpkin man? That was the most unsettling of all. It wasn't even possible for someone to fit a pumpkin over their head. And when it was back in his garden again, there wasn't even a hole in the bottom of it for someone to fit their head through. The whole thing was impossible.

What was even more impossible was that the pumpkin man was waiting outside his gate in the early hours of the morning. How could he have known that Gerald would be up at that time? Gerald hadn't even known that himself. The pumpkin man must have been out there a long time hoping that Gerald would get up and look outside. But that was ridiculous. Who would go to all that trouble? And why?

A more troubling question was whether or not the pumpkin man would come back again tonight.

But surely not. Gerald had smashed the pumpkin up really well. And why would he come back again? He'd already frightened Gerald once, so what would be the point of coming back again?

Gerald wished he hadn't thought of that.

R.I.P.

Gerald was restless all evening.

The pumpkin was now smashed more than ever, yet still he wondered if someone would glue it back together again. He tried to calm down, but he couldn't. He couldn't get his mind off the pumpkin, so he went through his usual evening routine of dinner, dishes then shower, but he did it all on autopilot. All he could think about was seeing the pumpkin man at his gate, coming home to find the pumpkin in his front yard, and discovering the time jump on his security recordings.

He was dying to check his security recordings to see if anyone was out there now, but he resisted. He also resisted peeking out from behind his closed curtains. Twice he'd almost looked out but dropped his hand from the edge of the curtain, asking himself if he really wanted to see what was going on out there.

In the end he decided to leave whatever was out there, out there. What he didn't see couldn't hurt him. So, no matter how great the temptation (and it was great) he didn't look outside. Instead, he watched TV for a couple of hours, but the whole time he was listening for any hint of noise from outside.

He went to bed exhausted, but sleep eluded him for a while. He'd closed his bedroom window before he got into bed, even though it was a warm night, to make sure he didn't hear any noises from outside. Eventually, he slept.

Gerald awoke from a sound sleep. Without even opening his eyes he knew it was still dark outside. He lay there for a while trying to will himself back to sleep, but the events of the last 24 hours kept playing repeatedly through his mind. He kept seeing the pumpkin man staring at him, coming home to find the smashed yet repaired pumpkin sitting in the middle of his front lawn, it's disfigured face now with a permanent scowl yet still distinguishable with its chipped lip. And then his own angry attack on the pumpkin, cutting it into tiny pieces. Feeling angry, yet at the same time, threatened and afraid.

Suddenly he heard a sound. It was so quiet it was hardly audible, but he heard it. It sounded like someone breathing through an underwater oxygen tank and mask. The sound only lasted for a split second, and it was very soft, but it made him jump.

His eyes shot open. He jumped again and took a hard intake of breath when he saw the pumpkin man standing at the bottom of his bed.

He let out a small involuntary "Ahh!" His heart hammered.

He sat up, his hands pushing hard against the mattress as he struggled to sit upright.

There was no one at the bottom of his bed.

What the hell just happened? He'd woken up with such a fright that it was hard to think. He was panting hard and shaking as he leaned sideways and attempted to turn on the lamp. His hand was trembling so much that he couldn't find the switch, and his fumbling nearly knocked the lamp off the small chest of drawers. But after a few seconds of panic, there was light in the room, which felt so much safer than being in the dark. His fear partially subsided.

It must have been a dream. He'd only dreamt he'd woken up and seen the pumpkin man in his bedroom and the fright had woken him up. But it had felt so real. It was hard to believe it hadn't really happened. Even though his logical mind knew that it was only a dream, his fear was real and wouldn't leave him.

He stared at his closed bedroom door, wondering what lay beyond it. Was the pumpkin man out there, waiting for him in the dark? Or was he even real? Gerald wondered if he was losing his mind and hallucinating the whole thing.

Right now, after getting such a fright, his need to go to the toilet was urgent, more important than anything else, real or imagined.

He needed to open the door and make it to the bathroom as fast as he could.

Moving quickly, so as not to give himself time to think about it, he threw back the covers, leapt out of bed, dashed to the door and flung it open. Hurrying as fast as he could without running, he raced through the house putting on every light in every room, his hands trembling the whole time.

Satisfied that he was alone, he went to the bathroom, then headed straight back to bed. It was just after 2 am, and he wanted to get back to sleep, although he doubted that would happen.

He lay there telling himself over and over that it was just a dream. But he kept the lamp on, just in case. As daylight began to creep in around the curtains, he dozed a little.

The next day at work he was exhausted. He'd thought about not going to work, but the thought of staying at home all day appealed to him even less. He didn't want to be alone. He sat in his office, grateful for all his colleagues that he could see in the bullpen outside his window. Usually, he was so focused on his work that he rarely looked up or even noticed anyone else there. But today it was difficult to concentrate.

He stared at his computer screen looking for a small error he'd made in the code of the day before, but his mind just wasn't on it. Coding errors seemed unimportant compared to everything else that was happening to him.

A knock on his door brought him instantly out of his reverie. He looked up as Aleisha entered.

She began with her usual smile that quickly turned into a frown. "Oh dear. What's wrong?"

Gerald wasn't sure what she was referring to.

"You look exhausted." She said.

Aliesha was his assistant as well as being a great programmer herself. He never needed her to "assist" with much, but they regularly sat together in his office to discuss the project they were working on and make sure the code was working correctly and look for ways to improve it or make it more 'user-friendly.'

Aliesha was in her late 20's, slim, blonde and pretty. Gerald found her pleasant to be around.

"I haven't been sleeping very well lately," he told her.

"I can tell," she said with a sympathetic smile. "I wanted you to take a look at what I've done. I've made a mistake somewhere, but I just can't see it, so I was hoping you could take a look for me, you know… fresh eyes and all that. But it's OK if you're not up to it."

"No, that's fine. To be honest, I can do with the distraction to help keep me awake. Bring me what you've done, and we'll take a look at it."

Aliesha smiled and went back to get her work. She sat in Gerald's office for the next hour as they poured over her code and she explained what she'd done, but the mistake she thought she'd made was still undiscovered.

Gerald sat back in his chair and stretched. "Let's go downstairs to the coffee shop and take a break."

Without hesitating, Aleisha stood up and said, "I'll get my bag."

The two of them headed off to the lift, went to the coffee shop, got two coffees and sat at a vacant table together, chatting the whole time about the project, oblivious to everyone around them.

To Gerald, it was the most relaxing experience he'd had in a long time, free from pumpkins, people wearing pumpkins, and sitting at home at night terrified about the next thing that might happen.

It felt so normal to sit and talk about his work, and Gerald loved to talk about coding, especially with someone as intelligent as Aleisha, who was also pleasant to look at.

They sat and chatted long after they finished their coffee. Aleisha took a notebook and pen from her handbag so that they could make notes and map out the problem.

Several pages later, Gerald had an epiphany, a true eureka moment when he solved the coding problem. He drew it on the page for Aleisha to see. They were both sitting close together, their heads bent over the page side by side.

Aleisha examined what he'd done and sat back with a beaming smile, clapping her hands excitedly. "You did it!"

"No, we did it," Gerald corrected her. "We've been going over this together for ages."

"OK then, WE did it, although I've been trying to figure this out on my own since yesterday."

That reminded Gerald of the problem he'd been trying to fix from the previous day too. "I was having a problem with my code yesterday too, quite similar to yours. In fact, I think this solution will fix my problem too."

"Win-win," said Aleisha, clapping her hands together twice as she said it. She looked genuinely happy for him.

"How long have we been down here?" asked Gerald.

Aleisha looked at the neat gold watch on her wrist. "Quite a while it seems. It's almost 12 O'clock. We'd better get back up before they all start leaving for lunch."

Gerald was feeling so relaxed and content he didn't want to go back to his office where he usually ate lunch on his own. Without thinking he said "Why don't we go somewhere for lunch together. My treat."

Aleisha looked briefly surprised, then smiled her usual happy smile and said, "Well, if you're paying...."

Gerald was surprised that he'd said it and stunned that she accepted. It only took him two seconds to get over the shock and reason with himself that the only thing that was about to happen was that he was going to have lunch with an intelligent and attractive colleague so that the inner calm he'd been feeling while in her company would (hopefully) continue throughout lunch. And it did.

He and Aleisha went to a nearby kitchen and bar where they ate toasted sandwiches and shared a bowl of hot chips. They also shared a jug of water while they ate, then afterwards they ordered two light beers and lingered over them as they chatted about their lives. And even though Gerald wasn't much of a socialiser, he found Aleisha to be easy company, and she had a positive attitude about everything.

She told him that she got divorced two years ago after a brief, and unhappy marriage of three years. She said she'd spent a few years studying hard at university to become a programmer while she worked part-time. That hadn't sat well with her then fiancé who felt somewhat neglected because she was always so busy.

After she graduated, they married and she was lucky enough to get a job straight away with a small up-and-coming tech company. She had worked long hours, which she didn't mind, but her new husband was livid.

She said over the next few years while she tried to advance her career, he began to belittle what she did for a living. When she was at home reading the latest computer magazines he'd ask her things like why she needed to read so much. Didn't she understand her own job yet?

Things got progressively worse until one day she quit her job and began working at her current job. The day before she started, she packed her bags while her husband was at work. She put all her belongings into her car and left without even leaving a note.

She'd already rented a room in a shared house with two people she already knew. She unpacked when she got there and started her new job the next day, at a place where her husband wouldn't know where she was.

Filing for divorce was her next step. It was easy. She asked for nothing from him. No property, no money. Just a divorce. Her lawyer did all the work, so her husband had no idea where or why she went or where she worked. It still took nearly a year to sort out all the nitty-gritty details before her marriage was officially over, by which time she already considered herself single.

"So," she concluded. "Although the marriage lasted four years, for the last year we never were together.

Gerald was impressed with her strong resolve to end the relationship as soon as she knew it was unreconcilable. "Didn't he ever come looking for you to ask why you left? Surely you must have run into him at some point!"

"No. I moved away so that we wouldn't run into each other. I didn't go far, just a couple of suburbs, but it was far enough. He works locally where we used to live, and I work in the city. I made it a rule never to go out for a night out in the city so that I never ran into him.

"Although," she said as an afterthought. "I did once run into him about a year ago. I'd gone to a bar after work to meet up with a couple of friends. I went to the ladies' toilet before I left, and as I came out, there was my ex, walking towards the gents.

"His jaw almost dropped when he saw me. I felt sick at the sight of him. He looked so happy to see me and said, "Aleisha..." I put up my palm towards him and said, "Don't," and walked away."

Gerald sucked air in between his teeth and said, "You are brutal in your rejection."

Aleisha sighed. "I have no reason, or need, to talk to him ever again. Having any kind of conversation with him would serve no purpose." She then changed the subject. "So, what about you? Any ex-wives in your closet?"

Gerald smiled. "No, none at all. I've always been single." He went on to tell her about his lifelong obsession with computer programs and living in Mount Eden. But he never mentioned Roger. Instead, he told her that the reason he moved to a suburb in Brisbane was because he got a job in the city. "So, you see, my life has been pretty uneventful compared to yours."

Aleisha laughed. "I wouldn't call a failed marriage eventful. But it did teach me to never get involved with a man who doesn't understand how obsessive we programmers are about what we do."

Gerald smiled and nodded in agreement. "I know what you mean. Even when I'm not at work I'm either reading about it or on a forum online chatting about it."

"Me too. What else do you get up to when you're not at work?"

Her question jolted Gerald back to his current problems because that was what was taking up all his time at the moment, and it was all he could ever think about.

Until now he'd felt relaxed and happy. A world away from his problems and just for a while, he could feel as though none of that was happening anymore.

But who knew what would be waiting for him when he got home.

*   *   *

Gerald was angry, so angry when he drove into his yard and saw the battered pumpkin sitting on his porch again. He was so sick of this stupid prank someone was playing on him.

They'd scared him before, REALLY scared him with the glued-together pumpkin and the pumpkin man standing at his gate in the middle of the night, but he wasn't afraid anymore. He was angry. How dare they keep coming onto his property and rummaging through his garbage bin. How they were messing with his security recordings he didn't know. Maybe they'd hacked into his account, but whatever they were doing, he'd had enough. He'd spent a pleasant few hours with Aleisha today and she'd made everything seem so normal again.

And now this. He needed to do something. He parked the car in the garage, picked up his shovel and stormed over to the porch. The pumpkin stared at him from its crazy, battered face. Despite the amount of hacking that Gerald had previously done to its face and the grotesqueness of its appearance, it was still recognisable from the nick in its mouth that was still clearly visible.

There was something evil and unsettling about its face, but Gerald's anger was greater. He swung the shovel and smacked the pumpkin off the porch. Despite his anger, Gerald was still afraid of the pumpkin and didn't want to touch it. He watched it roll across his neatly cut front lawn, coming to a stop a short distance from the place he'd found it the day before that was still smeared orange from his previous attack on it.

He dropped the shovel with a loud 'clang' and went to get his small axe. He set upon the pumpkin in a frenzy, hacking at it as hard as he could. He kept at it for what seemed like ages, cutting into the hard pumpkin flesh over and over until he was out of breath and the pumpkin was nothing but a pile of small orange, fleshy pieces.

Panting, he dropped the axe and sat on the lawn next to it, while he got his breath back. He stared at the pumpkin pieces. Surely he'd done it this time, made the pieces so small that no-one could piece it back together again. He also didn't want them to even try.

To make sure no one could take the pumpkin pieces out of the bin and glue them back together, Gerald picked up his shovel and began to dig a hole. He dug in on the already orange-smeared patch from yesterday.

Because he was unused to physical exercise, digging a hole big enough and deep enough for all the pumpkin pieces was a slow job. It hadn't rained in a while, so the ground was hard, much harder than he'd expected, but he wanted to do it right, to bury it deep enough so that no one could dig it out.

As he worked, he wondered who was doing this to him. Was it one of his neighbours? They were the ones who always knew if he was in or out. They were probably watching him right now, laughing at him. If they were, then hopefully he would see who it was. Maybe they'd do something to give themselves away. He glanced up often to see if anyone was watching him. Several of his neighbours were outside, but none of them were looking at him.

Eventually, he thought that his hole was big enough to hold all the pumpkin pieces. He'd hacked it into so many pieces that it no longer had any part of it resembling a face. He'd made sure of that. He'd hit the face with the axe many more times than he'd hit the rest of it. And even when the face was gone and all that was left of it was small broken pieces on the ground, he'd hacked at them all again and again. He wanted that face gone for good.

Using the shovel, he pushed all the pieces into the freshly dug hole. He nudged at them repeatedly until they were all in. He then shoveled the dirt over them. There was at least a foot of dirt on top of them all. When he'd finished, he jumped up and down on top of it to make sure its grave was nice and tight on top of it.

"R.I.P. you freak," he muttered to it, then picked up his shovel and axe and walked away.

A Friendly Face

Gerald had felt a gleeful amount of satisfaction when he stomped on the pumpkin's grave, yet once inside he still couldn't settle into his usual evening routine.

Someone had gone to a great deal of time and effort to scare him, and despite his attempts to stop them, they may not quit. Would dirty, buried pumpkin pieces be enough to make them stop? Surely, they wouldn't dig it up. Would they?

Perhaps some detective work was necessary. Later, after his shower, Gerald put on a t-shirt and comfy pants and went to sit on his porch to keep watch on his neighbours. If none of them were out there, then he'd just sit and relax and enjoy seeing the pumpkin grave, and make sure no-one came into his garden to dig it up.

When he opened the front door, he immediately let out an involuntary noise of surprise, that sounded like a combination of the word "ugh!" and a scream.

The pumpkin was on the porch looking at him. It was dirty, battered and scowling. He could even still see the chip in its mouth, so it was definitely the same pumpkin.

The pieces of it were so small and some were misshapen, so the pumpkin now looked somewhat misshapen too. Even the loose 'lid' and stem on the top of it had been glued back together and now sat at an odd angle because they were as malformed as the rest of it. The whole thing looked grotesque. He wasn't sure if its glower was due to the distortion of the pieces, or if its facial expression had somehow changed on its own. But surely a pumpkin didn't have feelings.

Gerald slammed the door shut.

"Impossible," his brain told him. Impossible that anyone could stick a smashed-up pumpkin back together again so fast. Impossible.

But he'd seen it.

With hands shaking uncontrollably, he switched on the porch light. His trembling hands were so out of his control that he hit the switch rather than press it.

He stepped across to the living room window and managed to grab hold of the curtain on the fourth try. Geez, was he scared. But he had to know. He had to see the pumpkin grave.

He waited a few seconds to try and calm himself and then pulled back the curtain just far enough so that he could see outside. The grave was open. It was a mess. It looked as though the pumpkin had burst out of it.

None of it made sense. Had the pumpkin escaped on its own? Did it put itself together before it burst out or after? Or did someone come and rip the grave open? The dirt was strewn all around the grave. It didn't look like someone had taken the time to dig it out. It looked more like an explosion.

He still couldn't understand how they did everything so fast. They must have been there immediately. Or was he dealing with a possessed pumpkin?

He let the curtain fall back into place. His trembling somewhat subsided, so he was back in control of his hands, even if they were still shaky.

He went to his study to check his security recordings. He rewound them to the moment he returned home. He saw himself pulling up on the driveway and the electric gate slowly closing behind him as the garage door opened. The pumpkin was on the porch.

He rewound the recording another hour, watching carefully. At exactly one hour before he arrived, the battered pumpkin appeared on the porch.

He leaned closer to his computer screen and rewound the recording slowly by one second. The pumpkin disappeared. The time had jumped back twenty minutes. Twenty minutes exactly. Even though he'd seen the unexplained time jump before, it still made him feel cold and uneasy.

He fast forwarded the recording to after he'd smashed and buried the pumpkin and gone inside, then slowed it down to only 2-times normal speed, watching for any hint of what was happening outside, a shadow or movement of any kind. It was a warm evening and there was no breeze, so the only thing that changed was the lack of light as the sun went down.

Neither camera showed the front lawn where the pumpkin grave was because they were concentrated on the front of the house, so very little of the front lawn was visible.

Nothing moved at the front of the house. Soon he was looking at a darkened screen because the sun had set. It looked so still out there, so how had someone dug up the pumpkin and glued it back together without even casting a shadow from the streetlight outside?

Suddenly, there it was. The battered and filthy pumpkin was on the front porch. He rewound it slowly. Just like before, there was a twenty-minute jump in time.

He continued fast-forwarding it slowly, all the while wondering how anyone could do so much in just twenty minutes. It wasn't physically possible. Was it? It must be possible though, because it had happened, but it wasn't possible because it was impossible. He could go crazy thinking about it. But he'd also thought that it was not possible to piece the pumpkin back together, yet someone had done it.

One thing he did know was that he was scared. If someone was trying to frighten him, they were doing a good job, but he didn't want them to see that he was afraid, although it was hard not to.

He kept watching the screen, hoping to see a clue somewhere. But still there was nothing. Eventually he saw himself open the door, look terrified, and close it again. So much for not showing fear.

Nothing happened outside after that and soon the recording had caught up with real-time, so now he was watching what was actually happening outside, which was absolutely nothing.

He sat back in his chair. What the hell was he going to do now? It was clear that no matter how many times he got rid of the pumpkin, it was still going to keep coming back.

He closed his laptop computer, went to the kitchen and got a cold beer from the fridge. He twisted off the top, took a few hard swigs from the bottle, and went to the living room and sat on the couch. He drank greedily from the bottle as thoughts about the pumpkin crowded his mind.

The bottle was soon empty. He went to the fridge for another one and sat at the kitchen table, turning the bottle round and round, trying to think of what to do about the pumpkin. He kept drinking then turning the bottle, his face a picture of concentration.

Maybe he should take the pumpkin far away and throw it over a cliff. But that would mean having to put it in his car, and he didn't want to do that. He didn't want to touch it at all. And it would probably be back on the porch in twenty minutes. Hell, at that speed it would probably get home before he did.

He sighed and took another big drink, almost emptying the bottle. The cold beer felt good going down his throat on such a warm night. But it didn't help solve his problem. There must be a solution, but he just couldn't think of it. He needed to get rid of the pumpkin permanently.

Or did he?

Gerald had a light bulb moment. What if he did nothing, just left the pumpkin right where it was, on the porch next to its grave.

The more he thought of it the more he thought it would work. So far nothing he'd tried had worked. The only thing he hadn't tried was ignoring it all. If he left the pumpkin on the porch, it would also stop whoever was doing it from coming into his garden again and again.

Gerald drained his beer bottle and went to the fridge to get a third one which he took with him to the couch and turned on the TV. He was so happy to have such a simple solution to what was becoming a terrifying problem.

He felt relaxed for the first time since he found the pumpkin on the porch four days ago. He watched a couple of comedy shows while he finished his beer, and then he went to bed and slept soundly, no longer worried about what someone may or may not be doing. To hell with them. Halloween would be over in a few days, and so would his problem, which he was sure, was no longer a problem.

The next morning he felt elated that he'd slept through the whole night without any Halloween-themed interruptions, or without waking up at all. As he stretched before he got out of bed, he decided that the best thing to do was to ignore the pumpkin and not even look at it, because he would only worry all day if he saw it, or worry even more if it wasn't there.

He didn't look outside as he opened all his curtains, and when he reversed his car out of the garage later, he kept his gaze fully on the car's reversing camera screen, swung his car out onto the road and drove away, eyes forward the whole time.

When he arrived at work the first person he noticed was Aleisha. She was sitting at her desk in the bull pen, and she smiled as he walked in.

For no reason that he could explain, he walked up to her desk and said, "Fancy going out for coffee this morning?"

Aliesha looked both surprised and happy.

"Love to," she said.

"See you at ten" he said and went to his office, aware that many people were watching him. Gerald rarely left his office and never went into the bull pen, so they were probably stunned that he not only went there, but to arrange a date.

Was it a date, he mused to himself. It was only for a coffee. Well, to hell with it. He didn't even know why he asked her, but he was glad he did. He'd enjoyed her company the previous day. She'd made everything seem normal again, and today he hoped that everything would be from now on. Maybe that was the reason for his out-of-character impulsiveness.

Just after ten o'clock Aleisha knocked and stepped into his office. She'd already had her handbag on her shoulder, ready to go.

Gerald looked up at the clock on the wall next to the door. He hadn't realised the time. With a quick glance through his window he saw that most of the others were gone already, or had a cup of coffee on their desks.

"Sure, let's go," he said getting up.

"Where we going?" asked Aleisha.

"I don't know," he said. "But somewhere where everyone else from here, isn't."

"Gotcha," she said.

They walked down the street, passing several cafes where they recognised colleagues. Finally, they came to one that only had strangers.

At the counter, there were two glass display cases. One contained hot food like pies and rolls. The other had different kinds of cake and slices. They each ordered a coffee and something to eat. Gerald paid and they went and sat at a vacant table near the back of the room.

The air conditioning was on despite the front door being wide open, but it was cool back there all the same.

Gerald found Aleisha's company to be now familiar and comfortable. He felt a schoolboy-type of crush on her. She looked happy to be with him, so he assumed she felt the same.

Aliesha looked around the room. "I've never been here before."

"Me neither."

Aleisha giggled. "That doesn't surprise me."

"Why?"

"You never go anywhere. You rarely leave your office apart from making a coffee in the staff kitchen or getting your lunch out of the fridge."

Gerald smiled. "I didn't know anyone was watching my habits."

Aleisha giggled again. "We don't have to watch you. We know where you'll be and when. We set our watches by you."

"Oh, come on," he laughed. "I'm not that predictable."

"If you say so," she said with a sly grin.

"Well, I'm definitely out of routine today, so everyone will have to set their watches some other way."

Aleisha leaned forward and said, "I'm surprised no one fell off their chairs in shock when you asked me for coffee this morning. But I'm glad you did. I enjoyed our last meet-up."

Gerald couldn't help but smile. "Me too."

He wasn't lying. He genuinely liked being with Aleisha and found her attractive too. If he was reading the signals right, she was attracted to him too.

They enjoyed having coffee and cake together so much that they completely forgot about the time.

Aleisha looked at her watch "Oh no, we've been here almost an hour. We'd better get back. I'm going to be in trouble."

"No, you're not," Gerald assured her. "You're with me and we've been out for a meeting together. THAT'S why it took so long."

"Will they believe that?"

"They have to unless they can prove otherwise. Anyway, we're paid for what we do, not how long it takes us, and we have been working together lately."

They both stood up and left the coffee shop together. Neither of them wanted their time together to end so they unanimously chose to stroll back to the office, chatting the whole way.

Later, Gerald wanted to have lunch with Aleisha but thought asking her might seem too pushy, so he went to get his food from the fridge in the kitchen and ate his packed lunch alone in his office as usual. When he finished his salad sandwich, he took his plastic lunch box to the kitchen to wash it out.

There were three people sitting at the tables in the kitchen. Two were looking at their phones and one was reading a newspaper.

None of them looked up.

As he walked back to his office, he saw there were perhaps only six people in the bullpen. None of them were Aleisha. So, instead of going back to his office, he went outside for a walk, telling himself it would do him good to get some fresh air when his real motive was that he hoped to bump into Aleisha.

Every time he passed a coffee shop or eatery, he glanced in to see if Aleisha was there while trying to act casual and not too obvious.

"Gerald!" The male voice made him jump and brought him out of his reverie.

A large, bearded man was standing in front of him smiling. Gerald felt that there was something familiar about him, but he wasn't sure what."

The man looked both surprised and happy to see him. "It's me. Brian."

"Brian Breezeman." Gerald's memory of him came flooding back. The two had known each other since school. They'd never been best friends, but they did hang out with some of the same kids and got along great with each other.

After school their lives had gone in different directions. From what he knew, Brian had become a solicitor and then a barrister and only came back to Mount Eden a few times a year. Gerald had seen Brian for a few years while he was still in Mount Eden, but had never seen him, or anyone else from his hometown, since he left nine years ago.

At first, he hadn't recognised him because of the beard. He'd been clean-shaven the last time he saw him. Now he had a neatly trimmed moustache and beard and was wearing what looked like an expensive suit. Gerald had only ever seen him in casual clothing before, but today Brian looked the part of a highly paid barrister. He was also carrying a stack of documents and a briefcase.

"So, this is where you're hiding these days is it?" asked Brian.

"Not hiding. Working."

"Still creating those amazing digital programs?"

"You bet. Still love it too. What about you? I can tell you're still an overpaid legal eagle," said Gerald, indicating Brian's clothes and briefcase. "But what brings you to the city?"

"My firm sent me here. One of the big companies is our client and their head office is here in Brisbane. I'm based in Sydney, but I'm up here for a couple more nights.

"Look, I'm kind of in a rush right now, but give me your number and I'll call you later. We can catch up over a drink. There's a bar at the hotel where I'm staying. It's not too far from the city. It's called Captain Adams."

Gerald laughed. "Oh, I know that place. It's near where I live.

"Even better. How about we meet there tonight and have dinner, say about 7.30?"

Spending time with Brian was the last thing he wanted to do. No doubt the subject of Roger's disappearance would come up. He'd moved to the city to get away from all his feelings of guilt about what happened, and he didn't want to talk about it now.

But Gerald wasn't good at coming up with excuses quickly. He couldn't think of an excuse to not go out for dinner, so he said, "Sure. That should be great."

Brian looked pleased. "Okay, give me your number, just in case, and then I have to go."

Gerald took out his phone. "What's your number?" Brian told him. Gerald put the number into his phone app and pressed "call." A phone began to ring in Brian's inner jacket pocket. The ringtone sounded like classical music.

Gerald ended the call. "There. You've got my number now."

"Thanks. See you at the Captain's at 7.30." Brian was already walking away as he spoke.

Gerald walked around the block and then went back to his office. He'd felt so upbeat before while looking for Aleisha. Now he felt despondent, dreading the Roger conversation that he knew was coming later. Usually, when people talked to him about Roger, and they all did because Gerald and Roger had been best friends, he said very little, terrified that if he said anything, he might say too much and incriminate himself. His guilt over not helping Roger when he fell, and not telling anyone what had happened, especially Roger's parents, was a heavy cross he'd had to bear for over ten years now.

So, he didn't want to start talking about it now. Maybe he'd get lucky and Brian wouldn't bring up the subject of Roger. But of course, that would never happen. Brian would probably want to give him updates on what everyone's suspicions were about what might have happened to Roger.

He tried not to think about it and attempted to lose himself in his work for the rest of the day, but it still plagued his mind. He looked at Aleisha out in the bullpen and wished he was going out for dinner with her instead.

When the workday was over he headed home. His thoughts changed to thinking about the pumpkin. He briefly wondered why both bad things were happening to him. Putting up with someone trying to scare him with a jackolantern was bad enough, but now he also had to endure an evening pretending that he didn't know what had happened to his friend.

Maybe these two things were karma. The pumpkin man had been dressed like Roger and now Brian was here to talk about Roger. So, it could be karma because it was all Roger-centric.

As he drove home, he thought that maybe what he should do was kick the pumpkin off the porch when he got home and then call Brian and say something came up, so he couldn't make it to dinner. That would be great. But he knew he wouldn't do either of those two things.

Gerald was almost home. As he turned into his own street, he picked up the gate and garage door remote controller from the centre console. It was one small device, programmed to the gate and garage door. He pressed both buttons as he swung into the driveway.

The pumpkin grave was still open, but the pumpkin was gone.

He drove in, parked the car in the garage, and wandered over to the front porch. The pumpkin was not there and was nowhere in sight. He looked in the grave. It was empty. He kicked the dirt back into it and stomped it flat.

He slowly surveyed the rest of the front garden. Nothing. No pumpkin anywhere. He went and checked the garbage bin. There was evidence that it had been in there from when he last cut it up and threw it in, but that was all.

So where was it?

The pumpkin had always returned before. But this time it was different. He hadn't cut it up, and he hadn't got rid of it. It seemed it had left of its own accord, although no doubt it would turn up again.

He walked into the garage, pressed the remote control on the wall to close the door and gate, and went inside the house, hoping that maybe, just maybe, the person taunting him with the pumpkin had given up. He thought about checking his security recordings to see when the pumpkin had been removed, but he didn't have time. It probably would only show him that someone had done the now-you-see-it-now-you-don't trick with a time gap that jumps ten minutes or so.

Right now, he had to have a shower and get ready to go out. He hadn't been out at night in a long time.

I'll Drink To That

Gerald wanted to shower and get ready to go out in a relaxed state of mind. But his life just wasn't that simple anymore. It was a long time since he'd been for a night out. A few times he'd had a drink after work with some of his colleagues, and a few times he'd been to the local pub for a meal and drink and watch the footie on their substantial big screen TV, but he wasn't big on socialising so on all those occasions he hadn't stayed long. Tonight he was nervous because he didn't want to talk about what happened to Roger, but at the same time it felt good to be going out to dinner with a friend. And he didn't have to stay long if he didn't want to.

But none of that mattered at the moment. What occupied his thoughts right now was whether or not the pumpkin would reappear, or, God forbid, the pumpkin man would make another appearance.

Gerald told himself he was being silly. The pumpkin man would never appear if there was a possibility that others might see him, he felt sure about that even though he didn't know why.

He closed all his curtains when he went inside then headed to the bathroom. After a leisurely shower and shave, he wrapped a towel around himself from the waist down and headed to the living room. Standing in front of the front window he took a slow, deep breath and pulled the curtain back just enough to be able to see outside.

He leaned forward and peered through the small viewing gap he'd created. The sun had gone down just enough so that it was still light enough to be able to see outside, but it was dark inside with the curtains closed so no one outside could see him. He hoped.

He let out a small sigh of relief that the porch was still empty. No pumpkin to be seen anywhere and the pumpkin grave still looked just how he'd left it.

He let the curtain fall back into place and headed to the bedroom, putting on a lamp in the living room as he went. He knew it was childish. But he always felt safer with a light on.

For his night out he chose a long-sleeved checked shirt that had a casual yet dressed-up look to it, and a pair of chinos. He always walked to the pub because it wasn't far and he didn't like to drink and drive, even if he'd only had just one or two drinks. And he enjoyed the walk.

After he was dressed, he went to the study and checked his emails and then looked at the security cameras. Nothing had changed outside except that it was darker. He looked at a few news channels online, checked the weather to make sure there was no rain forecast for that evening, and checked the cameras again. Still OK outside.

He closed his laptop computer, put on his shoes and socks, put on his watch, put his wallet, keys and phone in his pockets, and headed out.

He hesitated briefly as he opened the front door, felt relief again when the pumpkin wasn't there, and left, locking the door behind him, and leaving the porch light on, just in case.

As soon as he closed the gate behind him his fear vanished. It felt good to be doing something normal and to get away from the house for the evening. If the person with the pumpkin had plans of how they were going to torment him tonight, they wouldn't have planned on Gerald not being there.

He walked along the street looking at all his neighbours' Halloween lights and decorations in their front yards. Not all of them had decorations, but many did. Some of his neighbours had their curtains open so Gerald got a glimpse into their lives through their brightly lit windows. He peered in as he walked, watching them all enjoying normal lives. No battered pumpkins on their front porches.

He berated himself for even thinking about the pumpkin. He wanted to enjoy the evening and not let any negative thoughts ruin it.

He picked up his speed and continued to the local pub, enjoying looking in many windows as he went. There were plenty of others walking into town and constant traffic on the roads, so it felt good to be part of normal life.

When he got to the pub, he went straight into the bar room to get a drink. Brian was already in there, sitting at the bar having a beer.

He greeted Gerald as he walked in. "Good to see you again mate."

"You too," Gerald responded. To the young woman behind the bar who'd just walked up to him, he said, "A schooner please." There was a row of six beer taps at the bar where he was standing, each with its plastic logo on top proudly advertising the different brands. Gerald touched one to indicate his choice. The room was large and openly laid out with tables and chairs and several high bench tables with high stools nearer the bar itself. There was a door at the far end leading into the restaurant which was where families with children went to eat. Background music was playing unobtrusively. Gerald almost smiled at how no matter where he went, if there was background music it was always from 30 or 40 years ago. It was as though pubs, eateries, supermarkets and department stores never updated their music.

He paid for his beer, took a sip and said, shall we grab a table?"

"How about outside? There's a really big veranda outback. And it's a lot warmer up here than down in Sydney so it doesn't feel too cold. In fact, it's pretty warm."

"Sure, why not."

The two men headed outside, picking up two laminated food menus from the bar as they went. They chose a table for four at the edge of the veranda and sat opposite each other next to the railing.

Brian looked over the garden area at the back of the pub and said, "It's great to be back in Queensland. I miss it, especially the hot weather."

Although Gerald wanted to avoid the topic of their hometown, it seemed normal to ask about it. "Have you visited your family?"

"Not this trip. I need to stay near the city. Even when I'm finished work for the day, there's still work to do. I only just made it in time tonight because I was trying to finish up a few things. Even though it's Saturday tomorrow, I have a meeting with the client in the morning. How about you? Do you visit home much?"

"Not much. I'm always busy with work too and I have a life here in Brisbane now."

"I know what you mean. I'm married now you know."

"That's great. Any kids?"

"Yeah, four. Two boys and two girls. They keep me busy when I'm not working."

Gerald smiled. He was genuinely happy for Brian. "I'll bet they do."

"How about you, Gerald? Any family?"

"No. Still happily single."

Brian smiled at him, but it was a sad kind of smile. "You always were quite the lone wolf. You've never been the noisy chatty type. So, what've you been doing with yourself the last few years?"

Gerald felt suddenly awkward and didn't know what to say. He looked at his menu. "I've been eating whenever I'm hungry. Just like now. Let's order something."

"Good idea." The subject quickly changed to discussing all the items on the menu.

When they decided what they wanted, Brian went back to the bar to order it, saying he'd pay for it with the company credit card. "They don't want me to starve so they give me 'open season' on one of their cards, so I always live the good life when I'm out of town.

While he was gone Gerald went to the drink's chiller across the room. It was full of bottles of water. He opened the heavy glass door, took out a bottle, grabbed a couple of chilled glasses that were in there too, and took them back to the table. He sat down and poured them both a glass of water and drank half of it before Brian came back to the table, carrying an order number on a small metal stand.

"Ah, water. Just what I needed." He sat down, placed the order number near the outer edge of the table where it could be easily seen, and took a long drink of water.

They talked for a while about their jobs and how they'd both advanced their careers over time.

When their food came, they discussed Brian's marriage and children. Brian made light of how demanding being a parent could be.

When their meals were finished and the plates taken away by a young waitress, Brian headed back to the bar for more beers, saying. "I'm sure the company won't mind shouting us a couple more drinks."

When he came back with the two schooners of beer, they clinked the top of their glasses together which made a dull clunk, said, "Cheers," and took a sip each before putting their glasses on the table, almost in unison.

"So," said Brian. "When was the last time you went back to visit the old country?"

Gerald felt himself tense. "To be honest, not for a few years. I prefer people to come here if they want to see me, or we all meet in the city and have a day out or a weekend away."

"Sounds nice."

"It is. I prefer meeting on neutral ground. Even if the family come to my house, we all go out for lunch or something, you know, take the nieces and nephews to the park."

Brian laughed. "You always were a strange guy."

"What do you mean?"

"Most people want to invite family to their home, but not you. You try and keep them out."

Gerald smiled. "Yeah, I know. They have been to my place once or twice, but only for a few minutes then I take them out somewhere. I always consider my house as my sanctuary. It's where I go to get away from everyone, so I don't want to encourage them in."

Brian laughed and then looked serious. "I went back home to visit family a few months ago. I went with my wife and kid and stayed with my parents for a couple of nights."

"Sounds nice."

"Well, it was, and it wasn't. The kids certainly enjoyed it, playing with their cousins and it was nice to spend time with my dad, but the town is still different since Roger disappeared. Until his body's found, no one there will have closure, especially his parents."

Gerald's feelings of guilt came flooding back as soon as Roger's name was mentioned. He hoped it didn't show on his face. Thankfully, Brian was gazing out into the garden as he spoke.

"That doesn't sound good," Gerald said quickly.

Brian turned back to look at him. Gerald picked up his beer, drank, and put it down again, to see if his hands were shaking at all. Ten years ago, when Roger disappeared, Gerald's hands quivered whenever anyone talked about it, so he always had to hide his hands back then. Here with Brian, his hands seemed steady.

Brian talked about Roger as the two of them drank their beers. He said that no one could understand how a person could just disappear like that with no one seeing what happened, especially as Roger was fit and regularly walked the mountains, which was the only place where his body could be and not be found. And he usually walked and hiked alone, so if he had an accident, no one would know.

Gerald had heard it all before. It was the same conversation that everyone had ten years ago, only now it was clear that the only difference was that Roger was now presumed dead.

"I guess no one will ever know," said Gerald, unable to think of a better response.

"I wish we could know," said Brian. "I spoke with Roger's dad a few months ago. He said his wife, Roger's mum, had been ill for some time and didn't have long to live. He said she wasn't afraid of dying, but she didn't want to die without knowing what happened to her son. They'd accepted that he was dead a few years ago, but it's the not knowing that hurts them."

Gerald cringed at the news. He knew Louise and Jimmy well. Louise was a sweet and kind woman and was well-known and well-liked.

Gerald was the only person who could tell her what happened to Roger. But he wouldn't. Too much time had passed. How could he tell anyone that not only had he known all along what happened to Roger? But he'd watched him fall to his death and hadn't helped him? The awful vision was still so clear in his head.

Gerald suddenly realised that Brian was talking, but he hadn't heard a word he'd said. "People have even started walking up and down the mountains again, hoping to see some sign of anything. I reckon what they're looking for is a glimpse of Roger's body somewhere, but no one wants to admit it. Do you know there's still a missing person poster in the town square with a picture of Roger wearing the same clothes he was wearing when he disappeared, his red checked shirt and blue body warmer?"

Gerald's mind jumped instantly to the night he saw the pumpkin man standing outside his gate, wearing a red checked shirt and blue body warmer. Roger's clothes.

Recurring thoughts about the pumpkin man tumbled through his mind. How could that be? How could someone fit a pumpkin over their head? How could they know about Roger's clothes? Was the pumpkin man real or had he imagined him? Seeing the pumpkin man had felt completely real, and terrifying at the same time. It was the scariest moment of his life. But now he questioned it. At the time it seemed so real, yet impossible.

"Gerald? You ok?" Brian was looking at him, concerned."

"Oh, I'm fine. It's all just bringing back awful memories."

"Sorry. I keep forgetting he was your best friend."

"He was. It was never the same there without him."

"That's why you left?"

"That and a great job offer in the city."

"Of course. But Roger was such an active bloke, always outdoors, and you, well, you're the opposite. How did the two of you ever become friends?"

"I don't know. Probably because we had our own interests, me with computers and Roger with fitness, and we often preferred to do our own thing than hang out with the other kids who always seemed to be doing nothing much of anything."

"I guess that makes sense. But didn't you ever go on any hikes up the mountain with Roger? He must have asked you to come with him at least once in his lifetime."

Gerald could feel his hands starting to tremble slightly. He quickly hid them under the table. Some people were great liars, but Gerald was not, especially when it came to the subject of Roger's death.

"Look at me. I'm overweight and clearly not the outdoors type. Walking here tonight is about my limit when it comes to exercise. And I can't imagine why anyone would want to hike up a mountain. Doesn't seem like fun to me. And it's not even safe. We used to hear all the time about people falling and getting injured on those mountains." Gerald felt pleased with himself for dodging the question, so he didn't have to lie.

"Yeah," said Brian. "But they're mostly tourists who don't know any better."

"Or locals like me who aren't built for hiking."

Brian laughed. "Ok, I get it. It was a stupid question." Then he got serious again. "There have been so many people who've slipped and fell and needed rescuing, but Roger knew the tracks, so I can't imagine him falling. But where else could he be?"

Gerald had to agree. When Roger went missing, a mountain track was the most likely place, despite Roger's familiarity with all the local mountains. "Tracks do change on the mountains, and it can cause unexpected slippage even for the most experienced walkers. Chunks of rocks can even fall away without warning. Just look at Mount Tibrogargan and how much of it has eroded over the years."

Brian looked intrigued. "For a man who says he's never walked up a mountain, you sure seem to know about the tracks changing."

"I've just heard, that's all."

Their glasses were empty. Brian went to get them another beer. Gerald let out a long sigh, happy for the break in conversation.

When Brian came back Gerald changed the subject to Halloween, which was now only a couple of days away. "So, do you take your kids trick or treating?"

"Hell no. We don't go in for all that nonsense. Most people in our neighbourhood don't either. You?"

"Nah. Some of my neighbours do but not too many."

They chatted about neighbours while they drank their beers and laughed a lot. Then they both agreed to call it a night because Brian had a meeting in the morning so three beers were enough. They said their goodbyes and shook hands. Gerald left while Brian, who was staying there, went out back to the motel rooms.

While it had been nice to go out for a change, it was also nice that it was over. Socialising was exhausting so the walk home would do him good.

The pub was on the main road which was still relatively busy with traffic. But once he walked around the corner onto a side street, he was instantly aware of the noticeable quiet. There were no cars on the street and no people on the footpaths either. He was alone. All the houses had dark windows, so the only light was coming from the streetlights, which were so far apart that the dimly lit street looked eerie.

He looked back at the main street. A steady stream of cars passed by. He turned back to the side street that somehow looked even more dark and creepy by comparison. Why were all the houses in darkness? The houses probably looked darker because most of them probably had the main part of the house at the back, opening out onto the patio. That's the way they were designed these days. With a living room/dining room at the back of the house off the kitchen. But right now, that knowledge didn't make him feel any easier.

There was also the noticeable lack of traffic which made the street seem unsettlingly quiet. But it was a side street, not a main street so there probably wouldn't be much traffic.

The street itself had a wide footpath with a grass verge at the edge, separating it from the roadside gutter.

Gerald took a deep breath and told himself that he was being childish. It was just a street that he was used to only seeing in the daylight. It had been so long since he went out at night that he'd forgotten how different things seem in the dark.

He was also upset to hear that Roger's mother, Louise, was dying. He felt bad that the one thing she wanted to know was where her son's body was. Gerald was the only person in the whole world who knew the answer, but he couldn't tell anyone. Not after all this time. Everyone would hate him. He wasn't sure if keeping it quiet was a crime, so he didn't want to risk it.

He'd had too much to drink tonight to think about it now. He'd only had three beers, yet he felt slightly drunk. Usually having three beers at home didn't affect his sobriety, but people always said that tap beer was stronger than bottled beer, and right now he could believe it. And also right now, he had to get home and hopefully the walk would do him good and help clear his head.

He took a step forward and then another. The street was so quiet he could hear every footstep. He quickened his pace. Every step echoed back at him. The sound of his footsteps made him feel vulnerable. The noise of his own shoes meant that everyone within earshot knew he was there.

But he was being stupid. No one cared where he was. But it still bothered him. He'd spent so much time already being afraid of the pumpkin and the pumpkin man, he wanted to feel safe now that he was away from all that.

But he didn't feel safe. He wished he was back at the brightly lit pub with people all around him and plenty of noise. He'd been there only a few minutes ago, and now he was alone in this dark, empty street with no sound except for his hurried footsteps.

The image of the angry pumpkin's face rose in his mind. His pace quickened. The image was of the last time he saw it, looking so beaten and misshaped, its angry face resembling a car crash victim, looking at him with loathing, for what he'd done to it, and the nick in its top lip looking like a scowl.

Seeing it so vividly in his mind felt ominous. Would the pumpkin be waiting for him when he got home?

A sudden noise interrupted his thoughts. What was that? Gerald thought he could hear something. He slowed his pace and stepped lightly trying to listen to the other sound again.

Footsteps. The sound was footsteps echoing in the distance. It was hard to tell where they were coming from. It sounded like they were all around him.

The street was long and rose slightly in the distance. There were no streetlights between Gerald and the top of the hill, but there must have been one just over the rise because he could see the glow from it.

Suddenly he saw it. The tip of something was coming into view over the brow of the hill. The backlighting meant that whatever it was, he couldn't see the front of it.

A head. As it came more into view, he could tell that it was a person's head, and they were walking in the middle of the road for some reason. Even though the person looked completely black in the dim street lighting, he could tell that their head was large and way out of proportion to the rest of their body.

Gerald was still walking slowly as the horror of what he was seeing suddenly struck him.

It was the pumpkin man.

'No it isn't!' his mind screamed at him. *'It's impossible!'* Yet there it was coming towards him. *'Maybe I'm wrong. I can't see it properly yet.'*

The old saying, *'Be careful what you wish for,'* flashed through his mind. He'd wished he wasn't alone in this dark street. And now he wasn't.

Gerald stood there, frozen. Numbed in horror, he watched the pumpkin man, staring at it mindlessly, paralyzed. Ominous thoughts swirled through his mind, but he didn't hear any of them.

It was still too dark to make out the face, but it was definitely the pumpkin man, walking slowly, hands hanging limply at its side. No other movement except for the slow, steady rhythm of it repeatedly putting one foot in front of the other. The pumpkin man was still at least eight houses away.

Gerald wanted to run. But to where? And what if the pumpkin man followed him?

He was too overwhelmed with terror to move. He tried to tell his trembling legs to run, but they wouldn't listen. He glanced furtively back over his shoulder at the brighter lights of the main road, but they seemed so far away now.

He looked back towards the pumpkin man and was so shocked at what he saw that the blood drained from his face. He made a quiet sound of helplessness.

The pumpkin man was no longer walking down the middle of the road in the distance. He was much closer and was standing on the footpath.

With only a few metres between them, Gerald could see the snarling face even though it was in shadow. He could also see that the pumpkin man was once again wearing the same clothes that Roger was wearing when he died.

Even though he was more afraid than he'd ever been in his whole life, Gerald couldn't move, transfixed by what he was seeing. As he watched, the snarl on the pumpkin man's face slowly morphed into a mocking sneer, with the nick in its upper lip, opening wider.

A prickling sensation shot up Gerald's spine. He was on the razor's edge of panic. He couldn't stop staring at the now-open nick in its lip. His heart hammered in his chest as the realisation hit him. He stood there in numbed horror, taking in every detail of the pumpkin man.

All this time he'd thought that someone was taunting him about his dislike of Halloween. And he had wondered if he'd only dreamt about the pumpkin man being outside his gate that night because that was the only way to explain why it was wearing Roger's clothes. He'd wondered if his terrified mind had somehow mixed things up just because he was scared and because Roger had died just before Halloween.

But now, here he was, seeing the pumpkin man again, and this time there was no doubt that he was real. And it wasn't someone trying to scare him. It was Roger.

He was wearing Roger's clothes. And it wasn't a mistaken nick in its top lip, it was Roger's cleft lip. It WAS Roger.

As all those thoughts ricocheted through his mind in seconds, the pumpkin man slowly nodded as though he could hear what Gerald was thinking and was confirming that Gerald had now finally understood.

Imprisoned by fear and shock at the revelation of who the pumpkin man was, Gerald could only stand and watch as the battered, sneering pumpkin face came closer when the pumpkin man continued its slow walk towards him.

Where Am I?

There was a noise—a beep every few seconds—and then another beep and a smell—a chemical yet familiar smell. There was also the distant hum of voices, rattling metal, and squeaky wheels.

Where the hell am I?

Gerald tried to open his eyes, but his lids felt heavy. He was tired and wanted to go back to sleep. But his need to find out where he was and what was going on was more of a priority now.

As his eyes fluttered open he could see he was in a brightly lit room. A hospital room. He was laid on his back with his arms out of the covers and by his sides. There was a machine at either side of his bed. On the left was a machine that looked like it was regulating a saline drip that was attached to a needle in his left forearm. On the right was a monitor showing his heart and breathing, and it was attached to him under a hospital gown he was wearing. There was a plastic clip on his right index finger that was also attached to the monitor.

Gerald looked around the room and down at himself in the bed, taking it all in and wondering why he was there.

There was a small bedside cabinet beside him with a remote control on top, which he surmised must be for the TV which hung from the ceiling above the foot of his bed. There were two closed doors to his left, probably a bathroom and closet, and a large window and open door to the corridor on the opposite wall from his bed. Thankfully there was a closed

Venetian blind on the window next to the door, or he would have felt exposed. On the other side of his bed was an armchair, and against the far wall was a small bistro table and two chairs. It was a nice room. But why was he in hospital?

Boom! Just like that, the memory of his last few minutes of consciousness came screaming back into his mind, making his hands shake and his heart palpitate.

The dark, quiet street. The pumpkin man coming over the hill with his slow, menacing walking pace. The dark, creepy pumpkin face coming closer. It's black eye sockets glaring. The nick in its top lip coming into view and the realisation that it was a cleft lip. Roger's cleft lip and the pumpkin man was wearing Roger's clothes. The pumpkin man was Roger

He jolted at the memory, confusion filling his mind. Why would Roger do this to him?

Then more memories. Sitting in the bar, Brian telling him that Roger's mother was dying and wanted answers about her son before she died.

He lay there unmoving with a torrent of thoughts racing through his mind. Images of Roger falling. Moving to the city. Pumpkin on his porch. Smashed pumpkin, dark, empty eyes glaring at him. Happy times with Aleisha. Meeting Brian. Pumpkin man in the dark street. Waking up in hospital. With every flash of every image, he was hit hard with emotion. Confusion, fear, anger, happiness, and most of all guilt.

"Oh, you're finally awake."

The sudden voice brought him crashing back to reality. He'd momentarily forgotten where he was. A slim, young nurse stood in the doorway. She smiled as she approached his bed. "You've been quite the sleeping beauty." She picked up the clipboard that was hanging on the bottom rail of his bed, wrote something on it, hung it back up, moved next to his head and started fiddling with the machines. Without looking at him, she said, "How are you feeling?"

"Tired." His voice was soft and croaky.

She stopped touching the machines and smiled at him. "I'm not surprised after the nasty knock you got to the back of your head."

Gerald put his hand to his forehead. There was a bandage wrapped around his head.

The nurse went to the other side of his bed and poured him a glass of water from the jug that was there. She used a remote control for the bed that was laying next to him, adjusted him into a laid-back, sitting position and handed him the glass of water. "Here. Sip this. Don't gulp it. Your mother's here. I just saw her in the kitchen making coffee. I'll go get her."

As she left the room, Gerald took a sip of water as instructed. His mouth was dry, so the water felt good. He took a few more sips, then his mother came in.

"Gerald, I'm so glad you're awake."

He wanted to be glad to see her, but she looked concerned, and he didn't understand why she was there. "That's what the nurse just said." His voice was less croaky, and his throat felt clearer. "How long was I asleep?"

"Three days."

Gerald was shocked but said nothing.

His mother continued. "You were found in the street late at night with blood pooled around your head. The police thought you'd simply fallen because you still had your wallet, phone and keys. We've all been waiting for you to wake up so you can tell us what happened."

Gerald continued to sip his water. "Three days? I've been unconscious for three days? It feels like three seconds." The water hitting his stomach made him realise how empty it was. "Have you been here the whole time?"

"Yes. As soon as they called me that night, your father and I came straight here. But you didn't wake up, so the next morning we went home. I packed a few things for myself and used your house keys to go and get a few things for you as well, like toiletries, clothes and pyjamas. They're in the cupboard next to your bed. Your keys are there too."

"Thanks." Gerald's thoughts were still swirling as he took in all this new information.

"How's your head? They said you've got a fractured skull and fifteen stitches, but they say you'll be fine. The police have been coming here every day to talk to you. Do you know what happened?"

He couldn't tell her the truth. "No, not at the moment. Thanks for staying with me."

His mother touched his arm lovingly and said, "I couldn't leave you."

He smiled at her. "I thought the nurse said you were in the kitchen making coffee?"

"I was. Would you like a cup?"

"Sure."

"I'll be right back." She patted his arm and briskly left the room.

Gerald put his now empty glass back on the bedside cabinet and closed his eyes. If he'd been asleep for three days, then why was he so tired? He was asleep before his mother came back into the room with the two cups of coffee.

The tiredness continued throughout the day. He was woken many times with doctors and nurses checking his pulse, removing the monitors and all the lines attached to him, police trying to wake him, but he just kept falling back asleep. Nurses kept bringing him food and telling him he needed to eat. But all he wanted to do was sleep. So, he did.

He woke up early the next morning when a nurse threw back the curtains at the window next to his bed. "Good morning," she said cheerfully as his eyes opened. "It's nice to see you awake for a change."

She was a different nurse to the one he'd seen the day before. She was older and stocky. "What time is it?" he asked her.

"It's seven o'clock. Breakfast will be here in an hour. Would you like me to unhook you from the drip so that you can have a shower?"

"Sure. That would be great." As she unstrapped the needle and removed it from his arm, he said, "What day is it?"

"Tuesday. It's time you started moving."

"Yeah, I want to."

"But take it easy. Move slowly. You'll feel stiff after being immobile for so long, but that will soon pass. There you go. It's all gone." She patted his arm affectionately near to where the needle had been inserted and took everything with her when she left the room.

Geralds's bed was still in the laid-back sitting-up position, which made it easier to get out of bed than if he'd been laying down flat. The nurse was right about his limbs feeling stiff. It felt like he was recovering from a tough physical workout. He mused at how inactivity produced the same physical feelings as over-exertion.

He gathered his belongings and made it slowly to the bathroom. The shower felt great. By the time he'd finished in the bathroom, breakfast had arrived. He was famished. When he'd undressed for the shower, he'd noticed that he'd lost weight. He'd dressed in the pyjamas his mother had brought for him, and they felt loose. He sat on the edge of his bed, feeling clean and happy to be wearing his own clothes as he tucked into the food that had been left for him on a hospital tray on wheels.

He spent the day out of bed, mostly sitting in the comfy armchair next to his bed, wearing his pyjamas and cotton dressing gown.

His mother arrived mid-morning and stayed for a couple of hours. She brought him a few homemade snacks that he was grateful for. The hospital food was ok, but he also liked to eat whenever he wanted and not just when they brought him a meal.

Not long after his mother left, a woman wearing a blue kitchen apron with a nametag that read, 'Brenda' came in with a cup of coffee for him. She asked if he wanted sugar and milk. He didn't, so she smiled and left, saying she'd be back for the cup soon.

He'd only just sat back in his chair with the cup in both hands when two uniformed police officers walked in, one male, one female. The female was slim and looked like she was in her twenties. The male was thick-set and probably in his fifties.

"Gerald?" said the male officer. Gerald nodded. Seeing the police made him instantly nervous. He hoped it didn't show, but it probably did. The last time he'd spoken with the police it was about Roger's disappearance. He'd felt so guilty at the time because he'd lied to them and said that he had no idea what happened to Roger and that he hadn't seen him that day. Both those things were a lie, and he wasn't a good liar. Back then the police seemed to think that his nervousness was down to his being worried about where his friend was, and that had only made him feel more guilty. That was why he'd left Mount Eden, because he was lying to everyone, and he couldn't stand it. Now seeing the two police officers brought all those guilty feelings flooding back.

His guilt must have shown on his face because the male officer said, "Are you OK?"

Gerald put his cup down on the bed tray, hands shaking. "Yeah, I'm fine. It's just that waking up here with no memory of how I got here feels so weird. Surreal even. Then you two walking in made me feel worse. I'm just having a strange time right now."

"I can imagine," the officer said. "Do you mind if we sit down?" He nodded towards the small bistro setting across the room.

"Sure," said Gerald.

The two officers each picked a chair and brought them over to sit in front of Gerald.

The male officer said, "I'm Senior Sergeant Craig, and this is Constable Roberts."

The young female officer nodded and smiled at Gerald. He half-smiled back. "What can I do for you both?"

"We wanted to know what happened to you the other night," said Sergeant Craig, "but you said just now that you have no memory of how you got here. We attended the call a few nights ago and found you laying bleeding in the street. We figured it wasn't a robbery because you still had your keys, phone and wallet in your pockets. There was no one else around at the time except the person who found you. A door-knock was carried out the next morning, but no one heard or saw anything the night before. So naturally, we hoped that you could tell us what happened."

There was a pause. Gerald said, "Sorry. No clue."

Officer Roberts spoke next. "Hospital tests showed you had consumed a fair amount of alcohol that night. Had you been out drinking? Do you remember where you were earlier that evening?"

Gerald paused again. He didn't want to say too much. "Yeah, I was at the pub with a friend. We had dinner, a few beers, and then I left."

"You left?' said the young constable. "Didn't your friend leave too?"

"No, he was staying there. He was in town for a few days on business, so we decided to catch up."

"Where do you know him from?"

"I've known him for years since we were kids. He wasn't a close friend, but we grew up in the same place."

"Mount Eden?" she said.

Gerald was taken aback by the mention of his hometown. How did they know where he was from? "Have you been spying on me?"

She smiled. "We've been making enquiries about you these last few days, but it was your mum who told us a bit about you and how you moved to the city after your friend disappeared and was never found."

Gerald felt his spine stiffen. His lips tightened, and his head began to pound with tension. He couldn't do it again. He couldn't talk to the police about Roger.

His instant anxiety must have shown on his face. The young officer said, "I'm sorry. I didn't mean to upset you."

Gerald, with lips still tight, said, "I just don't want to talk about that. Ever."

Although Gerald was no longer looking directly at them, he saw them glance at each other.

Sergeant Craig said, "Well there's no reason to talk about it now. Let's get back to the present. Did what happen to you have anything to do with what's been going on in your life lately?"

Gerald released some of the tension in his body and looked him straight in the eye. "What do you mean?"

"Anyone been bothering you? Have you been threatened at all? We're trying to establish if this was an attack or an accident."

Gerald thought about it for a few seconds. As long as he didn't mention Roger, it was safe to tell them about the pumpkin, but not the pumpkin man or they'd think he was crazy. Maybe they could find out who'd been doing it.

"Well, no one has threatened me verbally, but someone has been trying to scare me."

"For what reason?"

"I have no idea, but it's going on for days."

Sergeant Craig had a writing folder with him. He opened it, took out a pen, opened the notepad to a fresh page, and said, "Start at the beginning."

So, Gerald told him the whole strange story of repeatedly finding the pumpkin, someone gluing it back together and even somehow interfering with his security recordings. It took a while to explain everything that happened, but it felt good to be able to finally tell someone about it. The burden of keeping it all to himself had been heavy, but now it was lifting, and these people might be able to find out more.

Sergeant Craig wrote copious notes as Gerald talked.

When Gerald finished talking, Sergeant Craig wrote for a few more minutes, then put his pen back in the inner pocket of the folder, closed the notebook, closed the folder and laid it across his lap.

He leaned forward, forearms across the folder and said, "Gerald, we already know much of what you just told us."

Gerald felt his whole body stiffen. What was he saying? How could they already know? Gerald thought he'd been telling them a whole new story, and now he felt somehow cheated. They should have told him what they already knew instead of allowing him to babble on about it for ages.

"How do you know?" He didn't mean to sound annoyed, but he couldn't help it.

"We've already spoken to your neighbours," said Sergeant Craig. "They told us that you hate Halloween, so they were surprised when they saw a Jackolantern on your front porch. All your neighbours corroborate your story of smashing up the pumpkin, but they all assumed it was your pumpkin, so they thought you'd lost your mind.

"But who was putting the pumpkin on the porch and who dug it up?"

"They all think it must have all been you because no one saw anyone at your place or saw any strangers around or strange cars. According to them, the only strange thing that was going on was you."

Gerald sat ramrod straight in his chair as he listened, lips tight, hands gripping the arms of the chair. Before he could respond a man in a white coat who Gerald thought must be a doctor came in, accompanied by two nurses and what looked like three medical students.

"Oh, sorry," said the doctor. "Didn't know you were busy." He turned as if to leave. The others turned too.

"Wait," shouted Gerald. "What do you want?"

The doctor turned back to him, clearly annoyed at being spoken to like that. "I was going to quickly examine you but never mind. I've arranged for a few tests for this afternoon. Someone will come and collect you at 1 pm." The doctor turned and left abruptly followed by his entourage, all hurrying to keep up.

Gerald hated so many people being in his room at once. He didn't want to talk to anyone anymore. He didn't trust the police and wanted them to leave. "I'm tired. Please go."

"We just have a couple more things to go over with you."

Gerald reached over to the bed, picked up the remote call buzzer, and pressed it. Almost immediately a nurse appeared. She looked surprised to see the police in there.

"Yes?" she said to Gerald, leaning over him and turning off the call light.

"I'm tired. I want them to go."

The nurse turned to the police officers who both threw their hands up in surrender, put their chairs back at the small table, and left.

The nurse watched them go then said to Gerald, "Anything else?"

"No," he said, feeling his body relax. "I'm fine now."

Gerald's coffee had gone cold, and Brenda hadn't come back for the cup as promised. But it didn't matter because he could hear a metal rattle of something being wheeled into the ward and a strong smell of hot food. Lunch must have arrived.

Gerald went around the bed, took out his phone and plugged it in to charge, wondering if he'd had any messages while he was unconscious. He then thought about his job and wondered if they knew what had happened to him. Well, he'd find out once his phone was charged, which at this moment was completely flat.

Soon his lunch was brought in and his coffee cup was removed by the woman who brought his lunch. She tipped out the cold coffee in the small hand sink by the door as she left.

Gerald put on the TV and found one of his favourite comedy shows to watch while he ate.

Before he knew it, it was one o'clock, and right on time an orderly pushing an empty wheelchair arrived to take him for his tests, which took up the rest of the afternoon.

When he was wheeled back to his room he went for a shower and shaved and then sat on his bed and checked the messages on his phone. Clearly, they knew about him at work. There were messages from several people, including his boss, telling him to take as much time as he needed to recuperate, and Aliesha saying it wasn't the same at work without him and to let her know when he was awake.

He smiled when he read her message. He was glad she'd got in touch. He messaged her back straight away saying he woke up yesterday and had tests today, but didn't know how long he would be in hospital.

Just as he sent it, a nurse came in and said she wanted to change his bandage. "I've been waiting to do it for hours. You were gone so long." She unwound the bandage, cleaned the wound on the back of his head and wound on a new clean bandage. "The doctor will have a look at it in the morning and hopefully you can keep it off and let your wound dry out."

"Good. I can't wait till I can wash my hair again. It feels greasy."

"Yeah, it is, but you still look cute," she said with a wink as she left the room.

Soon after the nurse left, dinner was brought in. He ate hungrily. Afterwards, he sat in the armchair watching TV. It soon got dark, but he didn't bother to turn on the lights, figuring there was enough light coming through the open doorway from the corridor.

A short while later, the room suddenly darkened. Someone was standing in the doorway.

He looked at them and smiled. "Aliesha. It's great to see you."

"I couldn't stay away once I knew you were awake." She looked genuinely happy to see him, and she smelled freshly showered.

She walked over and kissed him briefly. Gerald turned off the TV and turned on the lamp above his bed. "Come and sit down."

They went and sat at the small table across the room.

"I'd offer you a drink, but you know?" he said with a shrug.

"Oh, we'll have plenty of time for that later, once you've done your time here."

Gerald laughed. "It does feel a bit like a prison sentence, and I don't even know when I'm due for parole. How did you know I was in here?"

"Everyone knows. When you didn't show up for work the boss rang you. Your mum answered your phone and said you were unconscious. We were all worried. Thank goodness you're OK. You are, aren't you?"

"So far. Haven't got the test results but I feel fine except for my literal splitting headache and that I feel tired all the time."

He was so happy to see Aliesha. Not just because he liked her but because she was something normal in his life for a change. Even his mother being there hadn't seemed normal because he didn't usually see her every day. But Aliesha was something else. He wanted to see her more, and he had been doing just that up until a few days ago.

They sat and chatted happily for a while, but all too soon a buzzer sounded and there was an announcement that all visitors had to leave. They said their goodbyes, kissed each other, passionately this time, then Aliesha left, leaving behind a happy smiling Gerald.

After breakfast the next morning, the doctor returned with his entourage and just as the nurse had predicted, removed his bandage but told him to keep the wound dry because he had a lot of stitches. He also said that the test results were fine, but because it was a head wound, they wanted to keep Gerald in for observation for a few more days, which was fine by him because there were no pumpkins there.

His mother arrived mid-morning again and they had coffee together.

Gerald was feeling upbeat for the first time in ages, but then the two police officers arrived, and his mother left.

"Didn't we finish this yesterday?" He asked them sarcastically.

"Well," said Sergeant Craig, "I did say we had a couple more things to discuss with you."

Gerald leaned back in the armchair, threw his hands up in the air in an exasperated manner, and said, "Fine. Fire away."

The two officers pulled up the two chairs again and sat down.

"Firstly, we want to talk about your night out with your buddy."

Gerald stared curiously at Sargeant Craig. "What about it?"

"We visited the pub the next day, and the staff told us that yes, you were there the previous evening."

"Wait. How did they know who I was?"

"We gave them a general description and described what you were wearing. They remembered you because you were with a customer who was staying in one of the rooms. We knew you'd been drinking because we could smell it on you and the pub around the corner was the nearest place."

"How creative of you."

Sargeant Craig shrugged. "It wasn't hard. Anyway, your friend had no idea what happened to you after you left, but he did want to talk about something else."

"What?" Gerald couldn't imagine what Brian would have talked about that included him. Apart from that one night out, they never saw each other.

"Roger," said Sargeant Craig.

Gerald froze again. Although his body was unmoving, his mind raced as he tried to remember what he'd said to Brian that night. The subject of Roger had come up when Brian told him about Roger's mother, Louise, being gravely ill and wanting to know where Roger's body was before she died. But he was sure he hadn't said anything about Roger to Brian. Why would he?" It was a secret he'd been keeping for 10 years.

He sat there numb, trying to remember the conversation. The two police officers were staring at him, waiting for a response.

"What about Roger?"

"Your friend said you and he talked about Roger's disappearance years ago."

"It was mentioned the other night, but only because Roger's mother is dying."

"It was a bit more than that."

"So?" Gerald wanted to relax, to not look guilty, but he couldn't. He was unsure of what was said and wondered where these questions were leading."

"You talked about dangerous tracks on the mountains when there's slippage and part of the track slides away."

Gerald felt his heart speed up. "Why are you talking about this? What does it have to do with what happened to me later?"

"Nothing. It has nothing at all to do with it. But it is the second thing we wanted to talk to you about."

"Why? I don't understand the connection."

"Roger disappeared just before Halloween. It's 10 years ago exactly. No doubt you'll always associate this time of year with your best friend's disappearance. People always do."

"And on this 10th anniversary, according to your neighbours, you've been fighting with a Jackolantern every night. And losing. Then your friend Brian turns up and tries to talk about Roger's disappearance, and you don't want to discuss it with him and keep trying to change the subject."

Gerald's fingers were gripping the arms of the chair tightly. "Are you suggesting that I had anything to do with his disappearance?"

"Did you?"

"What makes you think I did?

"You ran away from a place where you'd lived all your life after your friend disappeared. Most people want to stick around because it's an open loop in their mind until the person is found. But you left."

"Oh, for goodness' sake. I left because I got a job offer in the city, and it was a year later."

"You didn't 'get' a job in the city. You applied for it to get away."

"Whatever you think."

"And now your friend Brian thought it strange that you didn't want to talk about Roger when back home, everyone else is still talking about it all the time."

"If you're trying to say that I had something to do with Roger's disappearance, your reasoning is tenuous at best."

Sargeant Craig ignored what he'd said. "But you did have things to say about dangerous tracks as though it explained away what happened to your best friend. Apparently, at the time, most people were suspicious about why you, of all people, Roger's life-long best friend, never wanted to discuss what might have happened to him."

"Gossip? That's all you have. Gossip?"

Sargeant Craig leaned forward, hands clasped in front of him. "What you just said is what we call deflection. I made a statement about your suspicious behaviour, and you try and turn the attention onto me."

Gerald was flustered and angry at being accused. "I don't care what you think. I want you to leave."

Sargeant Craig, knowing that time was running out and if Gerald pressed the buzzer for the nurse again, they'd have to go, said, "OK Gerald. Let me tell you exactly what we know about all this. You might have been unconscious for a few days, but we were busy the whole time."

His words gripped Gerald's attention. He couldn't move or speak. Panic seized him. A feeling of dread encased him as he waited to hear what Sargeant Craig had to say. He could hear his blood roaring past his ears as he waited for what seemed like a long time but was probably only a few seconds.

"After speaking to your friend and your neighbours, we were more than curious about you. We checked out the trails on the mountains where you used to live, and it turns out that those tracks are checked every week for any breakages. And it seems that a couple of days after your friend disappeared, only one spot on one of the mountains was found to have a fresh break at the edge, and it looked as though most of what had broken away had fallen down the mountainside.

"So, it was fixed that same day and recorded in the maintenance log, with no one mentioning it or thinking any more about it. So, a few days after that, when people started to wonder if Roger had slipped, they began walking up and down all the tracks, and this same edge broke away again from all the excessive people up there. But everyone assumed Roger couldn't have fallen there because it wasn't broken until they all started looking.

"But we asked to see the maintenance logs and found the record of only one place on one mountain by a large rock with white paint on it that had been repaired at the time your friend disappeared BEFORE everyone went up there to search for him."

Gerald sat ramrod straight, still saying nothing.

Sargeant Craig continued. "So, do you know what we did? We reopened the investigation and sent cadaver dogs to search the base of the mountain in the white rock area.

"It was hard going for the search team because it's thickly overgrown there, with ferns so big they looked pre-historic. But by the end of the day, Roger's body was found. He was pretty much just a skeleton, but he was still wearing the remnants of his clothes, his red-checked shirt, blue body warmer, and, of course, his expensive white trainers. He also still had his wallet. His phone, however, was a few metres back, right where he must have fallen, and it had smashed into several scattered pieces, which would explain why he never called for help. He couldn't."

Gerald still said nothing, shocked at the news that Roger's body had been found. The police had known this all along, and suspected him of being involved but had said nothing, until now.

"And do you want to know what the worst thing was? He hadn't died quickly. That's why he wasn't where his phone had landed. It seemed that despite having many broken bones, he'd still managed to crawl."

Sargeant Craig sat back in his chair, glaring at Gerald, who still sat straight and silent. "Do you see what I'm saying Gerald? If someone had been with him and seen him fall, they could have called someone, and Roger would still be alive." He paused for a few seconds. Gerald still didn't move or speak. He couldn't. The image of Roger hanging in the tree after he fell, his eyes staring directly into Geralds. He thought Roger was dead. He'd heard him bounce off so many rocks before he landed in the tree that he thought the fall had killed him. It hadn't been a death stare. Roger had been looking at him, probably screaming silently for help. But Gerald had walked away.

Sargeant Craig continued "Unless, of course, the person who was with him had pushed him and wanted him to die." He leaned forward again. "Did he call to you for help?"

Gerald jolted at the question. It was the first time that they had accused him outright of killing Roger. He could have honestly said no, Roger had never called out for help, but that would be an admission that he was there.

He felt overwhelmed with guilt, learning that Roger was still alive when he fell from the tree. How long had he hung there? Gerald hadn't returned until two weeks later. But he'd come back because no one had reported seeing Roger in the tree, so he wanted to know if he was still there.

Gerald had to carry the heavy load of guilt because he should've told someone straight away. Even if Roger was already dead, at least his family would know what happened to him. But they probably would have blamed him. And why not? He had spent the last 10 years burdened with remorse for not helping Roger as he fell. It was something that would haunt him for the rest of his life. None of this would be happening now if he'd called for help 10 years ago, which he should have done, even if it was too late to help Roger, which, it turns out, it wasn't.

"Shoulda-woulda-coulda! Shoulda-woulda-coulda," his brain admonished him.

It was too much. Everything was too much right now. The police had no evidence that Gerald had been with Roger that day. No one knew. And no one ever would. They were just sitting here trying to extract a confession of murder out of

Gerald. He finally found his voice. "Why would I kill Roger or not help him if he fell? He was my best friend."

This time it was Constable Roberts who spoke, "Oh I don't know. Jealousy maybe."

"Of what?"

"He was good-looking, slim, popular, athletic, successful, you know, everything you weren't"

Gerald couldn't take it anymore. He needed to get out of there. Get away from them, but he had nowhere to go, so he bolted to the one place they couldn't follow him. The bathroom. He locked the door behind him and sat on the toilet. Now what? He hoped they would leave, but there was no sound from the other room.

Soon he heard them talking to each other in just a whisper so he couldn't hear what they were saying. But he knew they weren't leaving.

Then he saw the red cord hanging down beside him with a tag on it that said, "Pull For emergencies." This was an emergency. His head was pounding with an oncoming headache, his mind screamed with too many thoughts at once, and the old feelings of guilt were rushing over him again.

He pulled the chord. It made a 'click' noise and a red light above the bathroom door began to flash on and off. Hopefully it was flashing above the outside of the door too, so they'd know he'd called for help.

Within seconds there was a knock at the door and a woman's voice said, "Are you alright?"

"Have the police gone?" Gerald shouted through the door.

"They're just walking out now."

Gerald waited just to make sure he wouldn't see them when he came out. "Are they completely gone now?"

"Yes."

Gerald opened the door. The young nurse who he'd spoken to after he'd first woken up in hospital was there.

She looked concerned. "Are the police bothering you? This is the second time you've had trouble getting rid of them."

Gerald was tired. So tired. "I just want to be left alone."

"I'll talk to the doctor about it. We can't have you being upset, especially after a head injury." She patted his arm affectionately. "Leave it with me."

When she'd gone, Gerald locked the bathroom door again and spent some time in the shower, enjoying the warm water cascading over his weary body and letting his tension slip away. For the first time since he woke up, he carefully washed his hair while trying to avoid touching the stitches in the back of his head. After he finished the shower, he dried himself and dressed in his pyjamas and dressing gown again. Then he cautiously opened the bathroom door, just a crack, to make sure the room was void of police before crossing the room, getting into bed and laying down. He didn't care how early it was, he was tired. He put the TV on to help drown out all the hospital noises outside his room, closed his eyes and was soon fast asleep.

Gerald slept peacefully for several hours then his sleep changed to tormented dreams of Roger falling and Gerald reaching forward just too late to grab him. He dreamt of coming home repeatedly and finding the pumpkin on his porch, its dark cut-out eyes staring at him accusingly. Over and over he'd come home and there it was, only in the dream he knew it was Roger because of the nick in its top lip just like Roger's cleft lip.

Then he saw the pumpkin man at his gate, wearing Roger's death clothes. The dream pumpkin man didn't just stand there, he tried to come in the front gate, but for some reason he didn't know how to open it and just stood there angrily rattling it instead.

Over and over the pumpkin man who was Roger (Gerald knew this in the dream for a fact) stood rattling the gate, while Gerald watched from his open doorway, terrified that the gate would open this time.

Finally, he dreamt of the dark street and the pumpkin man coming towards him again and again. Only in the dream, the pumpkin man was running at him, angry and full of hatred, and Gerald stood there, wanting to run, but frozen, unable to move.

Then the dream changed again. He dreamt he was laying in his hospital bed. It was dark except for a dim light coming from somewhere down the corridor.

A sudden thought struck him. Was he still dreaming, or was he awake? He looked around the room. It all looked the same as when he went to sleep except that the TV was off and the remote control was on the cabinet beside the bed, and not on the bed cover where he'd left it. Someone must have come in and turned it off. Or had he done it himself? He couldn't remember doing it but that didn't mean he hadn't.

He closed his eyes and tried to get back to sleep, but it wasn't going to be easy because his dreams had been disturbing. He couldn't stop thinking about what the police had told him that Roger was still alive when he fell out of the tree and hit the ground. The image of Roger hanging in the tree, staring at him, needing help, but Gerald had walked away. *"But I thought he was dead!"* he screamed silently to himself. But it made no difference to his guilty feelings. He also knew that as Roger was slipping over the edge of the mountain, he'd done nothing to help him. He'd only stood and watched him fall, then looked over the side of the mountain at Roger hanging in the tree, suspended by his armpits, and walked away. His mixed emotions raged inside him. He felt sadness for what happened to his friend, shame at himself for not telling anyone at the time, and now a new emotion of anger at himself for leaving Roger to die.

"But I didn't know he was alive!" It was easier when he thought that Roger was already dead when he walked away. Now he knew that he was the one who left him to die. He was angry that he knew that and angry that there was nothing he could do to change anything now.

What he wanted was for it all not to have happened, to make it just a false memory.

But it was real, and he felt he was to blame.

He took a few deep breaths and tried to think of something pleasant.

"What was that?" His eyes shot open. He'd heard something. It sounded like a footstep. Just one. He'd probably imagined it after dreaming about the pumpkin man in the dark street. He closed his eyes again. 'Step!' He opened his eyes. The sound was closer this time. And now there was somebody there.

A man was standing outside the open door to Gerald's room. But instead of being at the door, he was leaning against the wall on the other side of the wide corridor.

Roger! Even though it was dark Gerald recognised him straight away, still wearing his death clothes. His cleft lip was somehow clearly visible.

Gerald began to shake the moment he saw him, terrified of what he might do. Until now he'd appeared as the pumpkin man, but now he was Roger himself.

Gerald felt an immediate rush of adrenaline and panic as he watched Roger take a step forward then turn and walk away past the window. He could see him through the half-opened Venetian blind, fading away to nothing as he went.

Gerald lay there staring at the now empty corridor, numb, frozen, terrified, his stomach felt like it was full of feathers. He struggled to calm his hammering heart.

Then he jolted awake. A nurse was putting on the lights in his room. "Good morning," she said cheerfully. "Breakfast will be here soon so get ready." She left without waiting for a response.

Gerald lay there wondering what had happened the night before. Had he only dreamt that he'd seen Roger? Or had he seen him, then fainted? Thoughts bombarded his mind as he tried to figure out what had happened. He'd first thought he was dreaming, then he thought he was awake, and then he woke up. If that wasn't enough to make you crazy, then what was? Maybe the best thing to do was to not think about it at all. But either way, he thought Roger had been trying to give him a message. But what was it?

He showered before breakfast hoping that maybe he'd have a eureka moment while under the running water. But he didn't.

Not long after breakfast the doctor and his entourage came to see him. The doctor told him that they were worried that he might have a breakdown due to head trauma from his fall and police harassment that was upsetting him. He said that the police had been told to stay away from him while in hospital and the staff would not admit them anymore.

Gerald was relieved. He didn't want to stay in the hospital, but he could tolerate it if it meant the police couldn't question him. It would also give him time to relax and calm his fretful mind.

A short while later his mother came to see him and told him that Roger's mother had passed away peacefully in her sleep last night. Gerald was stunned by the timing of her death. Was that why Roger had been there the previous night? Did he fade away because he was at peace? Was he with his mother now?

"At least the police were able to tell her what happened to her son before she went," said his mother. "Maybe that's why she finally passed. At least she has peace now and that's what's important."

"Yeah." But Gerald was only half listening, his brain already overloaded by his thoughts of the previous evening and the meaning of it all.

After his mother left, he decided to spend the rest of the day relaxing and watching "stupid" TV to help calm his mental clutter.

He was enjoying his emotional downtime when he was pleasantly interrupted by a mid-afternoon visitor.

"Knock, knock. Got time to talk?"

It was Aliesha. He was so glad to see her and couldn't keep the smile from spreading across his face. "I'm so glad you're here."

"That's the thing about being stuck in hospital. Any distraction is welcome," she joked.

"Well, there is that" he agreed. "But I am glad you're here. Hey, how about if I get dressed and we go to the hospital café for a coffee and something to eat? I'm sure there must be one here somewhere."

Aliesha smiled. "There's also a pub in the next street. What if we go there instead.?"

"I can't."

"Why not? You're not a prisoner here, are you?"

"No, but...." Gerald had no way to answer that. She was right. He could leave and come back if he wanted to, and a couple of drinks at a pub sounded better than coffee at the hospital café.

Aliesha looked at him expectantly, smiling as she watched him figure it out.

"Let's do it," he said, smiling.

"Great. It's a date," she said clapping her hands together.

"Yeah, you're right," he said. "It's about time it was a proper date. Aliesha, would you like to go out for a drink with me?"

"If you're paying, I'm drinking," she said with a laugh. Then she cleared her throat and said seriously, "Gerald, I'd love to go out with you."

They smiled at each other like two teenagers. Gerald, embarrassed, quickly broke their gaze. "I'll get some clothes and get changed in the bathroom."

"You'd better be quick. Don't keep me waiting," she laughed.

Gerald gathered some clothes and headed to the bathroom, feeling excited. Whenever he was with Aliesha he felt good. And now he felt even better because all his problems were over.

Roger's body had been found, and his mother had passed peacefully once she knew. And he felt sure that Roger had appeared to show him that it was all over, including the pumpkin saga. He hoped.

Naturally, nothing was going to bring Roger back, but nothing could. That was the downside to it all. He just needed to accept that and to be OK with it. He knew that in time he would be. He had to be. He'd grieved over Roger long enough.

On the upside, he now had Aliesha in his life, and it seemed that she wanted to stay. She was beautiful, intelligent and funny. Perhaps Aliesha came into his life to help him move on, to stop him from dwelling on how Roger died. The new information about Roger's death had shocked him, but it didn't change anything about what had happened. He had to move on, and he had Aliesha to help him do just that.

"You'd best be quick," Aliesha called out, laughing again.

Gerald smiled. Yep, from now on, with Aliesha in his life, the only way was up.

END